KU-127-722

The battle in Abbey Lane

THE OTTERBURY INCIDENT

10 005473 16
00547316

THE OTTERBURY INCIDENT

BY C. DAY LEWIS

ILLUSTRATED BY EDWARD ARDIZZONE

THE BODLEY HEAD

LONDON · SYDNEY · TORONTO

The Otterbury Incident is an adaptation of the French film *Nous les Gosses*, and I am greatly indebted to S.N. Pathé Cinema for kind permission to use the plot of that delightful film as the starting point of my story.

C. D. L.

Printed and bound in Great Britain for
The Bodley Head Ltd.
9 Bow Street, London WC2
by Jarrold & Sons Limited, Norwich

First published by Putnam 1948
Reprinted 1958, 1963
This edition first published 1966

CONTENTS

LIST OF ILLUSTRATIONS

TO

JONATHAN FENBY

AND

RICHARD OSBORNE

CHAPTER I

THE AMBUSH IN ABBEY LANE

BEGIN at the beginning, go to the end, and there stop—that's what Rickie, our English master, told me when it was settled I should write the story. It sounds simple enough. But what was the beginning? Haven't you ever wondered about where things start? I mean, take my story. Suppose I say it all began when Nick broke the classroom window with his football. Well, O.K., but he wouldn't have kicked the ball through the window if we hadn't just got super-heated by winning the battle against Toppy's company. And *that* wouldn't have happened if Toppy and Ted hadn't invented their war game, a month before. And I suppose they'd not have invented their war game, with tanks and tommy guns and ambushes, if there hadn't been a real war and a stray bomb hadn't fallen in the middle of Otterbury and made just the right sort of place—a mass of rubble, pipes, rafters, old junk, etc.—for playing this particular game. The place is called 'The Incident,' by the way. But then you could go back further still and say there wouldn't have been a real war if Hitler hadn't come to power. And so on and so on, back into the mists of time. So where does *any* story begin?

I asked Rickie about this, and he said, "Jump right into the deep end of the story, don't hang about on the edge"—which incidentally was contradicting what he'd said first. "Start with the morning you kids had the battle and Nick broke the window," he said. When Mr. Richards calls us 'kids,' nobody objects:

he's a decent chap, as schoolmasters go; and it's quite true we're young—even Ted and Toppy aren't fourteen yet. But when Johnny Sharp and the Wart strolled past our ambush on the Incident that morning, and Johnny Sharp said in his sneering way, "You kids up to your games again? Flipping heroes, ain't we all?" our blood fairly boiled, as you can imagine. We may be kids. But it was us kids who raised more than £5 for the broken window, and us kids who tracked down a gang of crooks and incidentally were thanked in public by Inspector Brook. So there's the start of my novel. You've got to have a title before you can start, I mean, and personally I think THE OTTERBURY INCIDENT is a smashing title.

"Zero hour in exactly five minutes, thirty-four, three, two, one, *thirty seconds*. Synchronise your watches," ordered Ted, consulting his chronometer. It was one of those super Swiss jobs, with a stop-watch hand and two smaller dials, as well as the ordinary hands and numerals. Ted's elder brother, who was in the Airborne, had brought it back from Germany as a present for his last birthday.

At zero hour Toppy's company, with its tank, would start down Abbey Lane. Our job was to intercept them, scupper the tank and prevent it reaching the school gates, a few hundred yards to our right. In order to reach the school, it had to pass the Incident. Ted's plan, which he'd just explained, was pretty crafty, I must say. There was to be a fake ambush and a real one, on opposite flanks of the enemy's route. "Toppy's bound to expect an ambush at the Incident," Ted had said. "All right. We'll give him one. Eight of us, under my command, will be hidden among the rubble heaps. When I give the word, this party will attack the tank

Ted Marshall puts us in the picture

with automatic-weapon fire. Their objective will be to divert the attention of the tank-crew and the escorting troops from the main attack. George will take three men, and——"

"How can it be the main attack if he only takes three men?" asked Nick. Nick's always putting his foot in it. He's not been awfully bright since the bomb fell. It killed his parents, and he was dug out of the ruins himself. So can you wonder? Still, we liked him all right. After all, it took guts to come and play on the very spot where it had happened.

"It's the main attack," Ted explained patiently, "because it's the attack that's going to wipe out the tank. Our attack from the other flank will be just a diversion in force, see?"

"Diversion in force, Persian horse, nasturtium sauce," Charlie began to chant.

"Shut up, Private Muswell!" Ted isn't a big chap. I mean he's not a tough like Toppy. But when he says 'shut up,' you shut up j. quick. Most of us do, anyway. Ted turned to me.

"George," he said (I'm his second-in-command), "George, you'll take three men and the sticky bombs, and hide in Skinner's yard."

Well, my blood froze. Skinner's yard is directly opposite the Incident, on the other side of the road down which the enemy tank would pass. It has high double doors, and there's a sort of warehouse or workshop inside. Skinner is in the building trade—or was. It was a wizard place for an ambush, of course. We'd be absolutely concealed behind the doors, and be able to keep watch through a crack in them. The trouble was Skinner himself. He's a whacking great bad-tempered thug of a man, with an unshaven chin and little blue eyes. Once two boys at our school tried to get into his workshop place, for a bet. He heard them and chased them out with a rope. He didn't just chase them out of the yard, he chased them right up the lane, slashing at them. That's the sort of man Skinner is.

"But look here, Ted," I began to say.

"You needn't worry: he's out for the day. I—my Intelligence Service saw him going off in a lorry after breakfast, and heard him tell a chap he wouldn't be back till this evening. And I've discovered the double doors aren't locked. You can climb over and unbolt them from inside."

Nobody can say Ted isn't thorough. . . .

Well, he gave us some more instructions, and that was when he told us to synchronise our watches. Which most of us did by looking up over the roofs at the Abbey clock, because we haven't got watches. It was just at this moment that Johnny Sharp and the Wart came lounging along and made the opprobrious remark about kids.

I'd better try to describe this pair of blisters. Personally, speaking for myself, I always skip the bits in novels where they describe people: you know—"He had a strong, sensitive face and finely-chiselled nostrils," or "her eyes were like pools of dewy radiance, her lips were redder than pomegranates"—that sort of thing doesn't get one anywhere, I mean it doesn't help you to *see* the person, does it? But descriptions of Johnny Sharp and the Wart are important, as I shall relate in due course. I'll start at the top and work downwards.

Johnny Sharp wore a grey homburg hat, rather on the back of his head and cocked sideways, with the brim turned down in front. He had a foxy sort of face —narrow eyes, long thin nose, long thin lips; he grinned a lot, showing his bad teeth and a gold-stopped one on the left of his upper jaw. He had a loud check suit with padded shoulders, and a perfectly ghastly tie with large patterns on it like drawing-room curtains. He had two flashy rings on his right hand, and a habit of flopping this hand at you while he was talking. He was a narrow, wriggling sort of chap, from top to bottom; like a dressed-up eel. Or a snake. He always behaved in a cocksure way.

The Wart wasn't a bit cocksure. He had a round, pasty face, and eyes that slithered about when he spoke to people. He never wore a hat. His hair was Brylcreemed, bunchy at the back. He generally wore a bluish tweed sports coat, with two slits behind, and dirty, fawn-coloured flannel trousers very broad at the bottom and trailing over his down-at-heel shoes. Everything about him looked rather scruffy. His real name was

Joseph Seeds, but everyone called him the Wart because he had a huge wart on his right cheek with whiskers growing out of it. And because he was a wart.

He and Johnny Sharp were always about together. The Wart had lived in Otterbury all his life; but Johnny Sharp only turned up there towards the end of the war. They'd evaded war service because of weak hearts or something. Neither of them ever seemed to do any work: at any rate, they were always mooching about together and cropping up where they weren't wanted. As e.g. this morning at the Incident.

"You kids up to your games again? Flipping heroes, ain't we all?" said Johnny Sharp.

Ted flushed like anything. Charlie Muswell said, "Better than being a couple of spivs," and dodged behind a rubble heap. But they didn't try to catch him. The Wart looked a bit furious, certainly, but Johnny Sharp only grinned, showing the gums above his teeth, and cocked his hat still more to one side, and slouched off. You'd think he was actually proud of being a spiv. The Wart trailed off behind him, and they went and propped up the wall of a condemned house a hundred yards down the street.

It was awkward, their being so near, from the point of view of getting into Skinner's yard. However, Ted sent a chap to divert their attention, and while he was talking to them, I and my party hoisted each other over the double doors. I had Charlie, Nick, and young Wakeley with me. And of course the sticky bombs, in a strong brown-paper bag. Peter Butts (he's Toppy's second-in-command) used to make these with his chemical set. They don't actually blow up or catch fire, which might be a bit dangerous: but they're terrifically adhesive. They ought to be called limpet bombs, really. The rule was that, if you stuck two on the enemy tank, it was put out of action. You weren't allowed to throw them—that would have been too easy; you had to slap them on to the tank by hand. This used to cause arguments about whether a bomb had been placed on the tank properly, or whether it had in fact been thrown from a very short distance, say a foot away. What we needed was an umpire. In consequence of these arguments, and getting generally worked up by the battle, tempers were frayed and relations between Toppy's company and ours had become rather strained at the time I'm writing about.

There were still three minutes to go. We'd unbolted the doors, and made sure there was no one else in the yard. The door of Skinner's workshop was padlocked, so that was all right. I heard Ted say, "Stand to! Get to your positions! Keep your heads down, men, and put out those pipes and cigarettes!" A few moments later, I peered out between the doors. For an instant I thought Ted's party had deserted altogether. Then I began to pick them out, scattered over the bomb-site, one or two topknots showing above the rubble heaps; a wooden tommy gun sticking out round the corner of a blitzed doorway; one chap hidden behind a clump of willowherb growing in the ruins; another doubled up inside one of those concrete, roller-shaped things the Council had deposited there. They were wizardly camouflaged, believe me. I noticed that Ted had taken a couple of old derelict dustbins, which had been lying about amongst the ruins, and put them across the lane just to our left, so that the tank wouldn't be able to pass.

My party started to eat their iron rations (it was the dinner interval at school, I should have said).

"What'd I give for a square meal!" said Charlie, biting into his cheese sandwich.

"What'd you have," asked young Wakeley, "suppose we weren't on rations—I mean, suppose we weren't an anti-tank detachment operating in hostile territory?"

"I'd start with a tin of sardines, spread on thick-buttered bread. I'd go on with a plate of éclairs. Then I'd have a shepherd's pie—a whole one to myself—with roast potatoes as well, and beans. After that, a treacle tart, and then a double ice-cream with chocolate sauce. And a box of Milk Tray chocolates to fill up the chinks. What about you, Nick?"

"Oh, I dunno," said Nick, who was sitting on his football. "Same as you, I expect." He looked a bit miserable. The uncle and aunt he'd gone to live with after his parents were killed didn't treat him very kindly. Some people said they half starved him; but you know the way people gossip in a small country town like Otterbury.

"You take two of the sticky bombs, Nick," I said.

"What?—Oh, thanks awfully; but I'd rather have my football. I've tied a length of string to it, and I can use it to bop them on the head."

So I divided the bombs between the other two. There was only half a minute to go. My heart was pounding like mad. I wasn't really frightened, at least not much: it was the responsibility of commanding the main attack. "Don't come out too soon," Ted had told us: "wait till they're heavily engaged with my party. Otherwise the whole thing'll go off at half-cock."

Just then I heard the rumble of the enemy tank coming down Abbey Lane to our right. To be absolutely accurate, it wasn't a rumble, but a clattering, squeaking noise, made chiefly by the old tyreless bicycle wheels on which the tank ran. It was a wizard job, that tank. We'd built it in the school workshop. The superstructure was made of wood, and we'd dazzle-painted the sides: there was a bit of camouflage netting, which Ted had got from his brother in the Airborne, over the top of it, and a broom handle sticking out through a hole in the front for a gun. It held three people easily: the driver, who pedalled it; the gunner; and the tank captain. With its high, box-like shape, it really was more like an armoured car, but we called it a tank.

I flicked the safety catch of my tommy gun and peered out into the lane, expecting to see the tank come nosing round the corner. What was my consternation to see a couple of enemy cyclists instead! Toppy had sent them in advance to clear any obstacles there might be in the lane. Crikey, I thought, they'll shift the dustbins and the tank will have a clear run through! Heads down, the cyclists went charging past, straight for the dustbins. They were going to ram them. A tornado of fire broke out from the ambush at the Incident, but the cyclists went on through it, seeming to bear charmed lives. Then, just when I thought all was lost, the lids of the dustbins flew off, two heads popped up from them like jack-in-the-boxes, and two walking-sticks were pointed straight at the charging cyclists. Ted had manned the dustbins! The cyclists, frightened of getting a stick between their spokes or in the belly, swerved aside. One of them—his brakes must have been bad—went tearing on past the bins and didn't pull up till he was fifty yards down the lane. The other swerved to his right, skidded, bumped away over the Incident, and fell off into a heap of rubble, where he was pounced on by one of our chaps. The first wave of the enemy had definitely had it.

But Toppy wasn't beaten yet. The tank now

appeared, with a file of three men walking bent down on its left side, where they were sheltered from the fire of Ted's ambush—and, of course, between my party and the tank itself. The tank stopped, about ten yards down the road. Its gunner was blazing away at the ambush: the protecting file, taking cover behind it, began to blaze away too. Then I noticed Toppy himself, with three men, creeping into the bomb-site on Ted's left flank. Ted's party were so taken up with the tank that they didn't notice this threat. Toppy and his men were wriggling along behind the rubble heaps, trying to get in Ted's rear. The situation was definitely deteriorating. If Toppy succeeded, he would catch Ted's party in a pincer movement between his tank men in front and his own infantry attack from the rear. I didn't dare yell out to Ted about the enemy creeping up behind him, for that would have given my position away, and the element of surprise would have been lost.

I now had to make a difficult decision. Should I go for the tank at once, before Toppy's party was ready to attack? Or should I hold back for another minute, in the hope that the three enemy men protecting the tank, who were at present lying on the ground between it and my ambush, would be drawn out of position? We could tackle the three men *in* the tank; but we couldn't tackle all six. I decided to hold back my force a little longer—though it was a hell of a job, with Charlie breathing down my neck and young Wakeley trying to wriggle through my legs to see how the battle was going.

I'd just made my decision, when the Prune buzzed a half-brick at Ted. I should have said we'd made a strict rule against throwing stones during our battles, except at the tank, which could take it of course. It *would* be the Prune who broke the laws of civilised warfare. He's a stinking specimen, take my word for it. Anyway, he was one of Toppy's party, and I happened to be watching them just when the Prune picked up this half-brick from the rubble heap he was crawling over, and bunged it. It caught Ted, from behind, on the funny bone.

Ted is a peaceable sort of chap normally. But now and then he fairly goes berserk: like he did in the last round of the School Junior Boxing Championship, against Toppy, after being miles behind on points in the first two. He went berserk again now. He stood up, and blew his whistle. There was a sudden silence in the battle. He yelled to the two men nearest him to help him attack Toppy and his three. Then he gave the three short blasts on the whistle which were the signal for the rest of his ambush to close in on the tank. Then he turned round and went for the Prune like a runaway fire-engine.

I saw my opportunity had come at last. As our chaps charged out of the Incident, the three enemy soldiers lying behind the tank moved round to its other side, to intercept them, and the tank-men started tumbling out too. I slid through Skinner's doors and raced for the tank, my men close behind me. It was too easy. We had no opposition, except from the enemy cyclist—the one with the bad brakes who'd shot past the dustbins. He's a small kid, and he'd been sort of spectating the battle from afar off, dancing up and down and yelling his head off in excitement, like kids do. However, when he saw my party bearing down on the tank, he leapt on his bike and pedalled at us top speed. Quite plucky, I'll admit. But he hadn't a hope. When he came up, we dodged; then I gave him a push from behind, just to help him on his meteoric career, and he went whizzing by, up the lane, round the corner and out of sight, still hauling like mad on his brakes.

Meanwhile, Charlie and young Wakeley slapped their bombs on to the side of the tank, two each, and young Wakeley crawled underneath and stuck another bomb on its bottom—five being, incidentally, a record in our battles. What's more, the tank being now abandoned, Nick and I climbed up into it and got a grand-stand view of the fighting. Terrific scrimmages were going on all over the Incident. It was hand-to-hand fighting; everyone had chucked away their weapons, except two chaps who were having a duel with swords on a rubble heap. Bodies, locked in mortal combat, were rolling about everywhere: the air was rent with the screams of the dead and the dying. I saw Ted land the Prune a Joe Louis upper-cut, which tumbled him backwards over a rusty old drainpipe. Just then, Toppy blew his whistle, and all his men who weren't casualties began streaming back towards the tank. In the heat of the battle, the enemy hadn't yet realised that their tank was captured. As they shot past behind the tank, Nick leant out and bopped one after another of them on the head with his football, yelling out: "You're dead! *You're* dead! *You're* dead!" He got four of them like that, and last he got Toppy himself.

"What the hell are you playing at?" shouted Toppy.

"Lie down," I said. "Don't you know when you're dead?"

"*And* we've destroyed the tank," said Charlie. "We've put five sticky bombs on it, honest. Look."

"Oh, you have, have you?" Toppy said, when he'd examined the side of the tank, and underneath it. "Yes, that's O.K. Five bombs. The tank's blown to smithereens. And so are you two fools in it. And therefore Nick couldn't have conked anyone with his football. And *therefore* I'm *not* dead."

Well, as you can imagine, this started a proper argument. Both armies were jostling round the tank now, and everyone talking at the top of their voices. Personally, speaking as an impartial historian, I must admit that Toppy was right; but of course I didn't say so then. We were still arguing, and Ted, with his nose about an inch from Toppy's, was just saying, "You'll admit the tank *is* knocked out, and that was the objective, and therefore we've won," when the school bell rang.

I started pedalling the tank down the lane, with half a dozen chaps pushing. The rest rushed on ahead, dribbling Nick's football. I was just roaring through the school gates when there was an almighty crash and tinkling of glass. Someone had kicked the football slap through the big window of the classroom next the Headmaster's study.

CHAPTER II

HELL TO PAY

For a moment or two everyone was paralysed. Then the crowd broke and rushed for cover, as if an air-raid siren had gone. In ten seconds, when the Headmaster came out on to the steps, the school yard was empty. I was hiding in the bicycle shed with Ted, Nick, and some others. I saw the Headmaster examine the broken window, very deliberately. Then he turned round and spoke to the empty yard.

"Will the boy who broke this window come forward at once."

Dead silence. I'd no idea myself who had done it. I felt sort of excited, comfortable, and ashamed, all at once, as you do when someone else is in trouble. The Headmaster repeated his request. I noticed Nick begin to start forward; but Ted clutched his arm and held him back.

"If the boy who did this doesn't own up at once, I shall cancel the half-term holiday," said the Headmaster, in a positively deadly voice. Nick moved again, and this time Ted let him go. Nick walked across the yard, very slowly, his head down, like a chap who's been bowled out first ball walking back to the pavilion. Boys emerged from their hiding-places, till there was a crowd of us standing at a respectful distance behind him.

"It was you who broke the window, Yates?"

"Yes, sir," said Nick.

The Head inflated himself, like he does when he's going to make a speech. But, after a shrewd look at

Nick Yates owns up

Nick Yates, he seemed to change his mind.

"How did you do it?"

"I kicked my football through it, sir. By accident."

"Hm'ff. I should hardly suppose that you would do it on purpose. However. There's been far too much of this ragging about on school premises lately, and far too many breakages." The Head gave us all a nasty look. "You will have to pay for a new window, Yates."

Poor old Nick looked like a puppy with distemper.

"But, sir, I haven't any money," he said.

"You should have thought of that before you started breaking up the school," replied the Head. "I'll give you a week to pay in. If you haven't got the money, your par—— your guardians will have to stop it out of your pocket money. Now go to your classrooms, all of you."

By a strange coincidence, Nick and I were in the classroom with the broken window, for that period. It was a maths. lesson with Mr. Robertson.

"Good lord, how on earth did this happen?" he asked when he came in.

"Yates kicked his football through it," said the Prune. "The Headmaster has told him he's got to pay for the damage. I should think it's pounds' worth, isn't it, sir?"

"Well, Prune, as you're feeling so helpful, you can get a dustpan and brush and clean up the broken glass," said Mr. Robertson. Which put that foul Prune in his place all right. "And in the meantime, Muswell, take your rule and measure the window. . . . Try, if possible, not to sever the arteries of your wrists on the jagged edges. There might be awkward questions in Parliament if a boy bled to death in my classroom. . . . Right, what do you make it?"

"Six foot by three and a half, sir."

"Very well. Now take your exercise books and work out this problem, all of you. If a square foot of glass costs 4*s*. 6*d*., how much will it cost to replace a window six foot high by three and a half broad?"

It was a pretty easy one, of course. In a couple of minutes we all had our hands up, except Nick, who was staring in front of him like a stone image.

"What's the answer?" said Mr. Robertson, pointing at me.

"£4 14*s*. 6*d*."

"Quite correct. . . . I said *sweep* up the broken glass, Prune, not grind it to powder beneath your clodhopping feet."

"Plates of meat," murmured Dick Cozzens, who is an expert in slang.

"You'll have to lend Yates the money, sir," said Charlie Muswell. "He's broke."

"Not as broke as the window," said Mr. Robertson. And a pretty feeble joke too, but we all laughed, just to keep him in a good temper.

The next hour was a slack one—English with Rickie. English is my best subject, so I'm in the top form, with Ted and Toppy. I noticed them glaring at each other, and wondered if there'd be a fight afterwards. Rickie was reading to us, out of *The Three Musketeers*—not bad stuff, though a bit old-fashioned for my liking. You know that saying about great events casting their shadow before them? Well, Rickie came to the Musketeers' slogan, 'All for one and one for all,' and he fairly bellowed it out: he's a jolly good reader, I don't know why they don't get him to read for the B.B.C. instead of some of those types who sound as if their gobs were stuffed with cotton wool. Anyway, it occurred to me that this would be a good motto for Ted's company. Little did I realise then just how true it was going to turn out. And not for Ted's company only. Within the next twenty-four hours there were destined to take place the Armistice, and the Peace of Otterbury, and —but I anticipate.

After school was over, Ted and I walked home together. My people live in Abbey Close, and Ted lives with his grown-up sister who keeps a bookshop in West Street—that's Otterbury's main shopping street, just beyond the Close. We had to pass by the Incident to get there. Well, as we were approaching it, I saw the door of Skinner's yard begin to open. I pulled Ted in against the wall, thinking it was Skinner coming out and he might have heard how we'd used his yard for the ambush. A face stuck out of the door, glancing up and down the street in a furtive sort of way. Then Johnny Sharp emerged. He must have spotted us, for he walked straight up, baring his discoloured teeth in what he fondly imagined to be a smile.

"How's your dear sister Rose?" he said to Ted.

"She's all right." Ted was rather taken aback. "You don't know her, do you?"

"Why not?" replied Johnny Sharp, tilting his hat at an even more spivvish angle. "Why not? I can read, can't I? I can go into a shop and buy a book, can't I? Any objection? Nice bit of goods, your sister is."

Ted flushed, and started to walk on. But Johnny Sharp flapped out his hand and took hold of him by the top button of his coat.

"Say! What's the hurry? Running home to do your home-work?"

You could tell what a fearful outsider he was, because he talked in a put-on American accent; and, besides, anyone knows we call it 'prep,' not 'home-work,' at our school.

"Yes, real class your sister is. Too good for a school-teacher, don't you think?"

"She's not a school-teacher."

Johnny Sharp flapped his hand. "Don't be dumb, kid. I'm talking of that *Mister* Richards of yours—him she's fixing to marry."

"That's no business of yours," answered Ted.

"Oh no? But it's yours, chum, ain't it? You're the man of the house, see? You should put your foot down. You don't want this *Mister* Richards living in the family, standing over you every evening to see you get your home-work done, giving you double home-work, like as not? Cor suffering cats, you don't want that, do you?"

Ted looked a bit shaken. I suppose the idea hadn't occurred to him before. But he said stoutly:

"Rickie—Mr. Richards is a decent chap."

Johnny Sharp flapped his hand again. "Take it easy! Take it easy! Did I ever say he wasn't? All I'm telling you is you don't want a school-teacher about the place all the time, with his lesson books and canes and all. It ain't natural. Besides, he's got no dough. School-teachers never have. Not what I call dough." And he flipped his fingers, like a conjurer, into a pocket and flipped out a whacking great wad of notes and tapped Ted on the nose with it. "See what I mean, kid? Know what these are?"

"Bank-notes."

"That's just where you're wrong. They're fur coats and slap-up meals and the best seats at the flicks and may be a nice little sports car. *Mister* Richards couldn't do that for your sis. Take him a year's pay to buy her a bunch of flowers, I guess. Huh, he's no good. You want her to be a shop-keeper all her life?" He put on a sort of refined accent: "Ooh, dyar me, fraightfully infra dig., keeping a shup, how ken she do it!"

"Oh shut up! Come on, George."

We were just about to buzz, when the yard door opened again, and Skinner came out. His voice rumbled like a volcano.

"Look yurr," he said, "was it by any chance you little blighters who broke into my yard this morning?"

"Broke into your yard, Mr. Skinner?" I said.

"You heard me."

"No," said Ted.

"Oho! No, sez you." His bloated great figure seemed to swell visibly, as he whipped something out from behind his back. "The yard doors were unbolted when I got home, and I found this school cap inside. A King's School cap, see? Suppose you wasn't by any chance coming back to fetch it out on the sly?"

"Whose name's it got inside?" I asked.

"Not so fast, sonny," rumbled Skinner. "Where's *your* cap, may I make so bold as to ask?"

I pulled it out of my satchel.

"And yours?" He turned to Ted.

Well, we'd had it then. You see, I'd borrowed Ted's cap that morning, having left my own at school, as a distinguishing mark for the leader of the main attack, and Charlie had knocked it off my head by accident just as we dashed out of the yard, and I'd forgotten about it in the heat of the battle. Ted had gone a bit pale, as you can imagine, with that great bruiser glaring down at him. Then Johnny Sharp said,

"I can explain."

"And who the hell are *you*?" roared Skinner.

"Name of Sharp. I happened to be passing this morning, and I saw some boys ragging about. One of them snatched this kid's cap and chucked it up in the air—the way kids do—and it sailed over into your yard. They couldn't get it, because the door was bolted. So that's the way it was. No bones broken, mister."

Of course Skinner had to give Ted his cap then, though he gave him a pretty suspicious look with it, out of his piggy little blue eyes.

As we went off down Abbey Lane, Johnny Sharp muttered from the corner of his mouth, "One good turn deserves another, young Ted. Cheer-oh. Be seeing you."

Ted was silent for a while as we walked. At last he said, "What I'd like to know is why they pretended not to recognise each other."

"You mean, Skinner saying 'Who the hell are you?'

to Johnny Sharp, just after Johnny'd come out of his yard?"

"Yep."

"Perhaps they *don't* know each other."

"Don't be feeble-minded!"

"Well, couldn't Johnny have been in the yard for some nefarious purpose? Loitering with intent? Burglars do often make a reconnaissance before they actually crack the crib. And he peered around in a furtive way before he slid out, didn't he?"

"You're not such a fool as you look," remarked Ted, after chewing this idea over.

"Wish I could say the same for you."

He whanged at me with his satchel, and we raced off homewards. Thus ended the events of Tuesday, June the 10th.

Skinner turns nasty

CHAPTER III

HOW WE SIGNED THE PEACE OF OTTERBURY

THE next day, in break, I saw Ted talking to Nick. Ted made our secret sign—scratching his Adam's apple—which meant that I was to follow him at a distance. Presently the three of us were in an empty classroom. Nick looked very depressed. Have you seen a bullock wedged in a cattle-truck? That's how he looked—sort of meek and desperate, as if he was caught in something and didn't know how to get out. Of course he was. And how!

"Nick hasn't told his guardians about it," Ted began. "He funked it."

Then the story came out. When Nick had gone home last night, he had begun to tell his uncle about the broken window: but he lost his nerve and finally said it was another boy who had done it; and his uncle said that, if it had been Nick, he'd have thrashed him as well as taking away all his pocket money till the window was paid for. Nick's uncle had pretty well foamed at the mouth with righteous indignation, I gathered, and what can you do when grown-ups get like that and refuse to listen to reason? It's easy enough to talk about 'owning up like a man': but sometimes, when you really do mean to own up, you suddenly lose your nerve and start making up a story, and then you have to go on with it—particularly if you've had a thrashing the week before, as Nick had. I'm no believer in corporal punishment anyway; I'd like to find a boy who is. But I digress. . . .

"We've got to do something about it," said Ted. "Any suggestions?"

I thought for a bit. "Suppose we form a deputation, and go to Nick's people, and explain——"

"He'd never listen," Nick interrupted. "It's hopeless."

"Well, what'll you do?" I asked him.

"Run away from home, I suppose." The word 'home' set him off and he began to weep.

"Don't be a twerp," Ted said. "People always get caught when they run away, sooner or later. And you can't run away without money."

"I'll kill myself, then."

"Turn it in, Nick!" Ted punched him in a friendly way on the shoulder. "Look here, we'll all help. We'll think of something. We'll have a council of war at lunch-time. Give the call immediately after morning school, George."

Nick looked as if he'd been thrown a lifebuoy. That's why Ted is leader of our company, I suppose: when he says something can be done, you really believe it can.

So, after morning school, I began to whistle Lillibullero. It was our rallying call. The idea was that each member of the company, when he heard it, was to start whistling it too—all except Charlie Muswell, who can't whistle, but he's in the Abbey choir, so he sings it instead. We only used the call in a state of emergency, of course: it meant 'Rally at once to the Incident.'

When Ted's company were all collected there, we had the roll-call. Ted then climbed on to a rubble heap and made a speech, like the Captain in *In Which We Serve.* He told them what had happened to Nick. He said the motto of any decent company ought to be 'one for all and all for one.' He said we'd got to do something about the broken window.

Just then, we heard feet marching along the lane. It was Toppy's company. They halted opposite us. Toppy and his second-in-command advanced, carrying a flag of truce. They'd come to challenge us to a return battle.

"We don't want a return battle yet," Ted told them. "We've got something else to do."

Of course Toppy's lot all started to jeer us for being windy. Ted flushed, but looked more determined than ever, as he does. Then the idea came to him which was destined to write a new chapter in the history of Otterbury.

"Look here," he said, "you chaps can come in on this, if you like. We're going to help Nick Yates pay for the window he broke. He's in trouble at home about it, and——"

"Just a minute," Toppy interrupted—he's a tall, thin, whippy-looking chap, with a bit of hair always falling over his eye—"what's this got to do with us? We didn't break the window, did we?"

"No, not actually, but——"

"Well then. Yates doesn't do our impositions for *us*, does he?"

"He doesn't offer to bend over when one of *us* is going to be beaten," Peter Butts chimed in.

"That's not the point," Ted answered. "What I mean is, we all kicked the football really."

"You're crazy!"

"The Reverend Edward Pijaw will now address the Sunday School!" yelled Peter.

"You shut up, Butts!" I said, going up to him in a menacing way.

"D'you want to be laid out?"

A challenge to combat

"They're windy!" shouted the Prune. "Yellow Ted and his sissy-gang!"

A general fight would have started that very moment if Toppy, to everyone's surprise, hadn't bawled out to his chaps, "Pipe down, all of you!" Then he turned to Ted. "What d'you mean, we all kicked the football?"

"Well, we were worked up; we tore into the school yard in a bunch, dribbling the football and passing it to each other. Then someone yelled 'Shoot!' and Nick happened to have the ball then and so he shot. It might have been you, or me—any of us."

"That's *his* bad luck," said Peter.

"Yes, but look—if you shoot a goal in a soccer match, it's scored to your side. And the same way——"

"*You* couldn't shoot a goal from ten feet away with the goal-keeper blindfolded," said the Prune.

It was this, really, that turned the tide: for Ted is centre-forward of the Junior School XI, and everyone knows he's deadly when his shooting-boots are on.

"Don't be cheeky, Prune," said Toppy. He'd been looking rather abstracted, as he does when a bright idea is brewing up in him. He's a queer sort of chap, Toppy. Behaves like a tough most of the time, and then suddenly for no apparent reason he'll take quite a decent line. "You know, it could be rather wizard," he said, in a brooding sort of way—we were all gathered round him and Ted by now—"it could be rather wizard. These battles are getting stale anyway. Kid stuff. What a smack in the jaw for old Bellyache"—that's Mr. Warner, our revered Headmaster—"if we turned up on Tuesday, the whole lot of us, with the money." He put on the Head's voice—"What we must all strive for in this school, from myself down to the most junior boy, is the—ahem, ch'rrm—the corporate spirit. We must all be members of one big happy family. Muswell, you are not attending, take a hundred lines for gross insolence." Toppy flung the lock of hair back out of his eyes. "Yes, let's give him a dose of his corporate spirit. We'll form a Grand Alliance between your company and mine, Ted, and raise the money somehow. If any of you chaps doesn't want to volunteer, let him take two paces to the rear, and go and fry his face over a slow oven."

Peter Butts looked a bit mutinous; but only the Prune broke ranks, edging slowly away and trying to look as if he'd lost interest in the whole business. I said we must sign a Peace before we could have a Grand Alliance. So I was instructed to draw up the pact. I did it on a sheet of paper torn from my diary, but later it was copied out fair, of course—on a big roll of parchment stuff we pinched from the Art Room, and we made real seals for it with ribbon and sealing-wax. Here it is, anyway—a jolly good historical document, though I say it as shouldn't:

BY THESE PRESENTS

WE, Edward Marshall and William Toppingham, do declare a state of amity and alliance between our several armies, supporters and pursuivants, heretofore vulgarly known as Ted's company and Toppy's company, the said pact to be recognised hereinafter by the title of THE PEACE OF OTTERBURY, and to be binding upon the signatories and their supporters or pursuivants under pain of outlawry until such time as the pact or Grand Alliance aforesaid shall be declared null and void by mutual consent of the signatories or their accredited representatives.

Signed: William Toppingham
Edward Marshall.

While I was drawing up this document, I was vaguely aware of a feverish activity going on around me. In fact, when I brought it for Ted and Toppy to sign, they seemed a bit impatient—well, afterall, a declaration of peace *is* an important thing, yet they just scrawled their signatures without even bothering to

Toppy and Charlie at the pawnbroker's

read it. They were sitting behind a counter they'd made out of an old plank resting on two dustbins, and the warriors of the late belligerent companies were filing past them, one by one, each man fumbling in his pocket and putting something on the counter. There were two heaps, one of money, the other of contributions in kind—penknives, Minicars, balls, pencils, bits of toffee—you know, all the sort of oddments you keep in your pocket. When everyone had contributed (I gave a tanner and a broken water-pistol myself), we had a pretty good collection of stuff, and 4*s*. 8½*d*. in cash. As for Nick, you never saw such a 'Came-the-Dawn' expression as he had on his face. And I must say it was queer to think how only twenty-four hours ago, on this very spot, we'd all been fighting to the death; and now here we were, weighing in with contributions to the Common Cause—young Wakeley even offered to give his white mouse, which was a pretty good show considering he and the mouse were absolutely inseparable—and Ted and Toppy sitting side by side as if they'd never laid crafty plans to annihilate each other's armies.

Well, Ted was appointed treasurer, and it was agreed that Toppy and Charlie Muswell should take the toys, etc., in a satchel to the pawnbroker in West Street. As I say, there was a fair heap of them, some as good as new, and we thought they'd probably bring in quite enough money, together with the 4*s.* 8½*d.* in cash, to pay for the window. Which just goes to show. What I mean, dear Reader, is—to anticipate my story—that you shouldn't count your chickens before they're hatched. And yet, if our contributions in kind *had* fetched the balance of the money we needed for Nick, we'd have had none of the adventures we did have, and this story would never have been written.

Presently, Toppy and Charlie returned, looking rather cast down. Toppy chucked half a crown on the plank.

"That's all he'd give."

There was a general groan, and Peter Butts said, "You've been jewed!"

"He only offered two bob at first," said Charlie Muswell. "Toppy bargained with him like anything. Honestly. Beat him up to half a crown. Pretended to walk out in disgust. And the pawnbroker chap rolled up his eyes and said he'd be ruined if he gave us more than two and threepence. So we started to put the things in the satchel again. And the pawnbroker said Toppy ought to be called Moses because he could get blood out of a stone. But he absolutely stuck at half a crown."

Poor old Nick's face had fallen like a barometer before a storm. But he took it very well; said how decent it was of us to have done our best, and not to trouble about it any more, and so on. But Toppy—his eyes were fairly glittering—said, "We've not *started* yet. We're going to get this money if we swing for it!"

"Stealing is barred," said Ted.

"Who said anything about stealing? We're going to *raise* the money. There's twenty-four—no, Prune's not interested—twenty-three of us. And if twenty-three able-bodied chaps can't raise £4 odd, we might as well go and drown ourselves. Look, we've got till next Tuesday. We've Saturday and Sunday free anyway, and Monday's the half-term whole holiday. Listen, you saps, we'll hold Otterbury to ransom over the week-end."

"D'you mean a sort of flag day?" someone asked.

"There isn't time to make the flags," Ted put in. "Besides, you've got to get permission from the police for a flag day."

"And people won't buy flags except from pretty girls, everyone knows that," said Peter.

"Flag day my foot," said Toppy. He struck an attitude on top of the rubble heap where he was standing. "The country is suffering from a shortage of labour. O.K. We'll supply it. We'll offer to clean people's windows, weed their gardens, do odd jobs—see what I mean?"

One or two boys groaned. Someone said, "But

you've got to have ladders and sponges and stuff to clean windows."

"We can borrow them, can't we, my poor fish?"

"I don't know how to weed. I don't know a weed from a flower," said Charles Muswell.

"You're a drone, you dear little choir-boy," said Peter Butts. "A droning little Abbey drone."

Ted snapped his fingers excitedly. "Carol-singing! Charlie can sing."

"Me sing in the streets? Come off it, Ted!"

"Not by yourself, fool. Hands up who else of us is in the Abbey choir."

Three hands were raised.

"There you are, then. The four of you can practise. Get some other chaps from the choir to join you, if you like. Practise: then go round the town singing, on Saturday."

"But we can't sing Christmas carols in the middle of June."

"Well, sing something else. Hymns. Comic songs. Anything."

"That's just what I meant," said Toppy excitedly. "Everyone should do whatever he's good at. For instance, Dick Cozzens is a slang expert—R.A.F. slang particularly, because his brother's in it. Why shouldn't he offer to give chaps in the school lessons in slang? Twopence a lesson, say?"

The idea caught on now like a prairie fire. Everyone began talking at once, saying what they could do, making suggestions. It's extraordinary, when you come to think of it, how, once one person has started a thing, the rest follow him as if they'd been madly keen on it all along. Like sheep going through a gap. Or like a trickling river that becomes a flood and sweeps every obstacle out of its way.

For instance, one or two chaps had the bright notion of borrowing brushes and polish from home and setting up a shoe-shine stand at the traffic-light crossroad in West Street. Then someone pointed out that the weather was set fine, and people only wanted their shoes cleaned when it was muddy. So this bright notion seemed to have had it. But Toppy, who'd been looking thoughtful, suddenly burst out with, "We've got to *make* their shoes muddy, then." And various ideas were put forward for this, and boiled down to the most practical one; and this idea was worked out in detail—you know, like Boffins working away in a back room to make some invention absolutely foolproof. And the final touch was a brainwave from Peter Butts which—but I won't tell you yet how the idea was worked out, because it would spoil my next chapter. Read on, and you'll see.

So there we were, everything going smoothly, everyone getting more and more enthusiastic. Except the Prune; and even he couldn't tear himself away at first; he stood about on the edge of the crowd, trying to look as if he was above all this sort of thing. But public opinion was dead against him, and presently he did drift off.

The only real difference of opinion we had was about girls. It became obvious that some of the things we were planning needed girls to help, and some boys who had sisters about their own age wanted to bring them in on it. Others—specially Peter Butts—were frankly sceptical about this. He said that, once you let women into a thing, they always wanted to boss it; and anyway, Ted's and Toppy's companies had always barred girls. But Ted pointed out that the companies had now been disbanded, and were regrouped into one big organisation—at any rate, for the purpose of Operation

Glazier, which is the name we'd decided on for the week-end job (it was I who thought up this name, actually, a glazier being a man who puts the glass in windows)—so there couldn't be anything in the rules against enlisting a few girls. We had a vote on it, and it was decided by seventeen votes to six that a limited number of females, approved by the committee, should be asked to join. The committee, also elected by vote, consisted of Ted, Toppy, Peter Butts and myself.

Another question which arose was whether we should tell our parents about Operation Glazier, or bring in one of the masters—say Mr. Richards. We were pretty well unanimous against telling parents, the chief reasons being that (*a*) grown-ups are apt to make a fuss about any activity, however harmless, which is off the beaten track, (*b*) Operation Glazier would lose the tactical element of surprise if half the town knew about it before it started, and (*c*) it would be much more fun to do the whole thing off our own bat. It was agreed, however, that if anything went badly wrong, the committee should be empowered to call in Mr. Richards as an adviser.

Well, there we were, all the preliminaries settled and the plans laid. And it'll show you how the scheme had caught on when I tell you that several boys who were supposed to go home for lunch (most of us bring packed lunches to school) didn't get home till lunch was nearly over.

As the committee was strolling back to school, the Prune appeared again. He had a wooden box under his arm. It was a new box, about 1½ × 1 feet, with a lock and key. He said we could borrow this box to keep the money in. We asked him if this meant he'd changed his mind and wanted to be enrolled, and he said yes.

I thought it was a bit odd. But the box would be useful, and we couldn't very well refuse the Prune's offer. So the box was handed over to Ted, as our Treasurer.

And if Ted had been able to see into the future at that moment, he would have taken the box and filled it with stones and dropped it into the deepest pool of the River Biddle—yes, my word!—Ted wouldn't have touched that box with a barge-pole. But, not being a crystal-gazer or a prophet, Ted put it under his arm, and we walked on.

CHAPTER IV

OPERATION GLAZIER

THE morning of Saturday, June the 14th, dawned bright and fair. This is not just a piece of novelist's padding: it is scientifically accurate—I know, because I was so excited that I awoke early. The birds were kicking up a fearful shindy in our garden (it is called 'the dawn chorus'); I got up and looked out of the window. The sun was just rising. Otterbury lay asleep, with that hazy look which promises a fine day to come, oblivious of the great events soon to disturb its ancient calm. The Abbey tower rode the morning mists like a galleon's poop. Zero hour for Operation Glazier was ten o'clock, when the housewives of Otterbury would have begun their shopping.

For this chapter I shall use historian's licence. A historian can't be everywhere even when he's writing about contemporary events. He pieces together documents, eye-witness reports, etc., and makes a coherent narrative from them. One advantage I have over the ordinary historian is that I don't have to bother about a lot of dates, which are sickening things, to my mind, and quite unnecessary. It all happened over the week-end. First, a great victory; then the moment when disaster stared us in the face; then the recovery from this crippling blow and the turning of the tables on a dastardly enemy: looking back on it now from the historian's viewpoint, I can see how events were divided into these three phases. As I say, I didn't actually witness all the happenings related in this chapter, but I shall write as if I had been present at every point of the battle. So here goes. . . .

At ten o'clock on the dot, a vehicle rumbled out of Abbey Lane into West Street. You would hardly have recognised in it the tank which, a few days before, had run the gauntlet at the Incident. A ladder was laid along its superstructure: instead of the gun, a long-handled mop protruded from the front turret; and on its sides, in large white letters, was printed:

KWICK-KLEEN CO.

THE RELIABLE WINDOW CLEANERS

Why have a gloomy view of things? We will brighten them up for you at the cost of only 6*d. per window. Just try us!*

The vehicle passed slowly along the whole length of West Street, and then back again, the buckets inside merrily rattling. Two boys were pushing it, and a girl was pedalling. Every now and then they stopped, and the girl stood up inside the vehicle and looked around. She was Charlie Muswell's sister. She's supposed to be pretty; and it was Toppy's idea that the window-cleaning party should have a bit of sex appeal. After showing themselves off to the morning shoppers, they moved away to the residential part of the town. They chose a house whose windows looked dirty, and rang the bell. Of course they got a raspberry sometimes. And sometimes some fearful hag appeared at the door and drivelled over them—"Dear little children! What a lovely game you're having"—that sort of thing. Which was pretty riling, as you can imagine. But they stuck to it, and got several jobs, particularly when some of the early-morning shoppers, who had seen them in West Street, returned home. . . .

At ten o'clock on the dot, the music started up. Charlie Muswell had got together a jolly good choir, eight of them in all, including three chaps' sisters.

Operation Glazier in action

They started outside the railway station, to catch people who were taking the 10.25 express to London; and they sang 'Casey Jones,' which is a song about a terrible railway accident that took place in America, for the benefit of these passengers. They were pretty nervous at first, and I don't blame them: after all, singing in the Abbey is one thing—people can't very well boo you there; but singing in public, in the street—well, it takes a bit of nerve, you must admit. However, they'd practised really hard in the evenings, and one of the girls was wizard on the banjo, and a boy played the drum to keep them in time; and though I'm not musical myself, I thought they sounded super. The concert party moved from one place to another in the town, generally singing only one song each time. This was partly to avoid trouble with the police. It was amazing the way a crowd collected wherever they sang: it might easily have caused an obstruction if they'd stayed long anywhere. Things didn't go quite smoothly for this party either. One or two young oafs started following them around, bawling out "What's it in aid of?" and other opprobrious remarks. Of course, Charlie Muswell and his boys could easily have laid them out, but if there had been a breach of the peace, the concert party might have had to pack up. However, the trouble was got over finally when Johnny Sharp turned up with the Wart, and warned the oafs off. Which shows that it's an ill wind which blows nobody any good. . . .

At eleven o'clock, the focus of activity moved to the Recreation Ground. This is a rather scruffy sort of public garden, between the station and the Abbey, with a few rusty swings and flea-infested sandpits for kids to play in. You generally get quite a lot of kids and

Miss E. Toppingham, R.A.

grown-ups there, though, on Saturday mornings. So a troupe of acrobats, led by Peter Butts who is super at gym., appeared and began a routine of tumbling, pyramids, etc., varied by exhibition boxing bouts and ju-jitsu demonstrations. Nearby, a table and two chairs were set up, with a poster saying:

Is Your Face worth a Shilling?
Lightning sketches by Miss E. Toppingham, R.A.
Sixpence only for children under twelve.

Toppy's sister is not an R.A., as it happens. But she's a smashing artist, and it was sporting of her to take this on, because she's nearly seventeen. Presently, Charlie Muswell's concert party arrived and sang several songs, giving the acrobat troupe a rest. Then Peter and Charlie took the hat round.

We'd had some argument about this. Obviously a lot of people would ask what we were collecting the money for, and we didn't think they'd be likely to shell out if we said it was for a broken window. Toppy was in favour of using a real charity—the S.P.G. for instance, which actually means the Society for the Propagation of the Gospel, but whose initials could secretly stand for our own charitable object too, i.e. the Society for Paying for the Glass. However, Ted was against this. He said it was too like chizzing, and in any case complications would probably arise later when the real S.P.G. heard about it. It was finally decided that we should say the collections were in aid of the N.Y.A.F., meaning the Nick Yates Assistance Fund: and if anyone got nosey, we should tell them it was the National Youth Association Fellowship. This solution of our problem was typical of the British genius for compromise. Ted thought it a bit crook, and voted against. But Toppy pointed out that, if any contributor was such a fool as not to know that there was no such body as the National Youth Association Fellowship, he deserved to lose his money; and anyway, since we were genuinely collecting for a charity, and not for ourselves, it was the spirit of the thing that mattered and we were entitled to practise a little harmless deception for a good cause. Being an eloquent bloke, Toppy won the vote on this. As an impartial historian, I must record my verdict that it was a case of the end justifying the means. . . .

What were Ted and Toppy doing themselves, while the acrobats tumbled and the choir sang and the window-cleaners cleaned? Come with me to the traffic lights in West Street. On the pavement there is a stool with brushes and tins of polish handy. SHOE-SHINE *3d.* Ted and I were operating the brushes in turn. We had a scout on either flank, to give warning if a Copper was coming along, because there's some law against plying your trade in the street without a licence. We could snatch up our stool and brushes in a moment, and carry them into Ted's sister's bookshop, which was only two doors away. But there aren't many Cops in Otterbury, and we weren't troubled that morning.

But how comes it that the shoe-shine is doing so brisk a trade on this fine dry summer morning, you are asking. Why, there's Mr. Richards coming down the street, his shoes polished like silver, not a speck of dust on them! He has poshed himself up to call on Ted's sister, Rose. He pauses a moment in front of her bookshop window, pretending to inspect the display there (but really I bet he's using it as a looking-glass). He moves on to enter the shop, but happens to glance down. Great Scott! His shoes are dirty! He looks round as if to find the puddle he must have stepped in. No puddle in sight. Most extraordinary. But there's a shoe-shine stool.

"Hello, you two, what on earth are you doing?"

"Shoe-shine threepence, sir."

"All right. I seem to need one. But what's all this about? Are you doing it for a bet?"

"Will you swear not to tell anyone, sir, if we let you into the secret?" asked Ted, after a slight pause.

"Yes, of course. If it's nothing criminal."

"We're making money to pay for the window Yates broke. The shoe-shine's only one thing. Other boys are cleaning windows, and we've got a choir, and a troupe of acrobats, and——"

"Well I'll be damned!" exclaimed Rickie. Which

The Flit-gun crew

shows how startled he was, because he's not usually addicted to oaths or imprecations in front of his pupils. "Hmm. It seems a worthy object. Good luck to you all. Hullo, here's the Headmaster! I wonder if *his* shoes need cleaning. I'd advise you to keep your heads down if he does come this way. He mightn't altogether approve of King's School boys working as boot-blacks."

Rickie gave us his threepence, and walked to meet the Headmaster. Not only that. He took old 'Belly-ache' by the elbow and steered him to the bookshop window. We heard him say, "Have you seen this new Naturalist's series? We ought to have it in the school library." And then, "Great Scott, sir, you must have stepped in a puddle somewhere! Look at your shoes!"

"Well! I could have sworn they were clean when I put them on this morning," said the Headmaster.

"I see there's a shoe-shine stand just there."

"Ah, yes. To be sure there is. Much obliged to you,

Richards. Yes, by all means order those books for the library."

And old 'Bellyache' came up and placed one of his trotters on the stool, and I kept my head well down as I polished, and he never noticed who it was.

Rickie had given us something like a wink, as he directed the Headmaster to our shoe-shine stool. There are no flies on Rickie. I'm pretty sure he'd spotted how his own shoes got dirty, and deliberately brought the Headmaster to stand in front of the window. You see, the bookshop has a basement, with a grating which opens on the street just at the level of your ankles. Toppy and another chap were standing on a table in the basement; they had a pail of muddy water beside them, and one of those Flit guns loaded with it. Whenever anyone stopped in front of the window, they sprayed his shoes with the dirty water, through the grating. It was a wizard scheme; and pretty well foolproof, because, in the noise of traffic at the cross-roads, our victims could never hear the hiss of the Flit gun —and in any case the sort of people who stare in at bookshop windows are much too absorbed to notice even if someone falls down dead at their feet. . . .

At midday some other boys relieved us on the shoe-shine stand. Ted, Toppy and I walked around to see how the other parties were doing. Toppy's kid sister (not the artist one) tagged on, which was rather a bore at first but turned out a godsend. It happened like this. We were strolling through the market place. Otterbury's market day is Thursday: but there are a few stalls and cheap-jacks there all through the week. Well, we noticed one chap trying to sell those curling-tong contraptions which girls use for their hair. I suppose his partner must have gone off for a drink. He must have *had* a partner, anyway, because he himself was totally futile at selling things—the reason being that he had a stammer like an engine missing on three cylinders.

"Bub-bub-bub-bub-buy a s-s-s-s-set a-whoo a-whoo a-whoo cuc-cuc-cuc-cuc--cuc-cuc-cuc urling tongs," he bellowed. "Gug-gug-gug-gug-guaranteed to gug-gug-gug——" etc., etc.

Well, naturally you can't do a roaring trade like that. Suddenly Toppy ducked through the handful of people at this stall, dragging his kid sister after him, and emerged behind the counter. The cheap-jack fellow's voice conked out altogether, so startled was he by this intrusion. Toppy lifted his sister up on to the counter (I should have said, she's got a head of bee-yootiful golden curls, which she's apt to toss at you in the way women do). Then Toppy seized a pair of curling-tongs, jumped up beside her and started an incredible flow of patter.

"Ladies and gentlemen! I have here the wonder of the age, Colley's Guaranteed Quick-Curl! Going at a great sacrifice! For one day only, one day only! Half a dollar a set, only half a dollar! All the rage in London and Paris! Ladies, one application of Colley's Quick-Curl Hair-Beautifier and you won't know yourselves! Look at this young lady here! Never uses any other. Do you, Madam?" He gave his kid sister a pinch on the bottom. "*Do you, Madam?*" "No," she yelped; then tossed her curls and began simpering at the audience in a revolting manner. "What an advertisement for Colley's Quick-Curl! Absolutely genuine, ladies and gents, ab-so-lutely genuine!" Toppy gave her curls a smart yank just to show they weren't a wig. "Now then, who will be the first to take advantage of this staggering offer? What about you, sir?" Toppy pointed at a rustic who was gawping in the front row. "Give your young lady a Colley's Quick-Curl and she'll be at the altar with you to-morrow! Come along, sir, don't be shy! Nothing venture, nothing win! Half a crown, and the girl is yours!"

And by gum the rustic did step up, his face the colour of beetroot, and put down his money. Toppy muttered something in the cheap-jack's ear—no doubt he was bargaining what percentage of the profits he should get—and the cheap-jack nodded, and Toppy was off again on his patter. The crowd round the stall was increasing every minute, and obviously in great good humour now, and there seemed nothing to stop Toppy unless his voice packed up; so Ted and I left him to it.

We set a vague course for the Recreation Ground, to see how they were getting on there. On the way, we ran into young Wakeley; he'd been weeding somebody's garden and looked even dirtier than usual, if possible. There was a blind beggar standing in the street where we met. An old lady came walking by, and we moved aside to let her pass, so that Ted and Wakeley were up against the wall on either side of the beggar. The old lady stopped, turned back, peered short-sightedly at the group, and said to the beggar,

"And are these your poor little children, my good man? What pretty boys! What a shame! Begging in the street! T'ch, t'ch, t'ch!"

Ted and young Wakeley were wearing their oldest clothes, and Ted had smears of boot-blacking on his face and hands, and Wakeley looked as if he'd been burrowing in the earth; so you can understand how the old lady made her mistake. The beggar was pretty quick in the uptake, I must say. And I bet he wasn't blind either. Because he piped up at once, in a sing-song whine, putting his hand on Wakeley's shoulder.

"Too true, lady. This is my youngest—Eustace. And this 'ere young shaver"—he seized Ted by the ear —"this is Cyril. The happles of their old dad's heyes, ma'am. All I have left, ma'am, since me old woman died. Poor motherless babes. Not had a bite of food since yesterday. Spare a copper for me starving kids, lady," etc., etc.

Ted and young Wakeley, the poor motherless babes, were red in the face and fairly writhing in the beggar's iron grip. But the old lady forked out a bob, clucking over them like a broody hen. When she'd passed on, the beggar gave Ted a frightful leer, and said hoarsely,

"Give yer sixpence if ycr stays 'ere beside me for 'arf an hour, you two nippers."

"Sixpence *each*," Ted put in firmly.

"Cor stone the crows, 'ave a 'eart, young gents. I'm a poor man——"

"Sixpence each."

"Call it ninepence for the pair. Split the difference, chum."

"Sixpence each," Ted replied. "Dash it all, we got that bob for you."

The beggar rolled up his eyes to heaven, groaned, and gave in. So I left them to it.

On the way to the Recreation Ground, I had to pass E. Sidebotham. It's a newspaper shop in a side street, where some of us get our Comics and Detective Magazines. It suddenly occurred to me, why not offer to take round E. Sidebotham's evening papers today? So I popped into the shop.

E. Sidebotham is one of Otterbury's most eccentric citizens. In fact, he's balmy. But quite harmless. A big man, with an untidy sort of face and an absolutely bald head, always talking to himself. Whether it comes of reading all his own stock of Bloods, or what, I don't know. But he's got a delusion that he's Sherlock Holmes: my father, who knows Inspector Brook quite well—the Inspector is head of the Otterbury police—says that E. Sidebotham is always pestering the police with offers to solve murder problems; not local ones—we haven't had a murder for years—but national ones. When I went into the shop, he had a button in the palm of his hand and was gazing at it through a magnifying glass.

"Highly significant," he said. "Take a look at this. Notice anything peculiar?"

I said I didn't.

"The trained eye perceives at once that the button has been *wrenched* off," he went on in his thick voice. "Observe the fraying of the threads. Now then, what does that mean? I will tell you, in one word. Violence." His voice sank to a blood-curdling whisper. "Maybe, *murder*."

"Where did you find it, Mr. Sidebotham?"

He tapped the side of his bulbous nose with a finger the size of a sausage. "A-ha! A pertinent question. The button—let us call it Exhibit A—was found by me at precisely nine and a half minutes past six, last night, on enclosed premises, while I was delivering newspapers." I suppose the word 'newspapers' was like a knell to toll him back to his real self. Anyway, as if a switch had been moved, he changed suddenly from Sherlock Holmes to E. Sidebotham: his eyes sort of unglazed, his voice altered, he put his hands on the counter and said,

"What can I do for you, young man?"

I asked if he'd let me take on part of his paper-round that evening. He was a bit surprised; but I explained we were collecting money for a charitable object, and he then said O.K., he'd give me sixpence to do it. It didn't seem a great deal, but I haven't got Toppy's and Ted's bargaining powers: so I accepted. He told me which streets I was to deliver the evening papers in. As I left the shop, he was taking up the button and the magnifying glass again.

I will pass over the remaining activities of that day. The various parties were hard at work throughout the afternoon. It had been fixed that we should all rendezvous on the Incident at six o'clock. I was a bit late, the newspaper-round taking longer than I expected. When I arrived, the rest had assembled and Dick Cozzens was telling the story of the film. We'd agreed—those of us who got money to go to the Saturday matinée at the movies—to hand it in to the Nick Yates Assistance Fund instead. But, in case anyone's parents should ask about the film we were supposed to have seen there, it was arranged that Dick Cozzens should go to it, and tell the story of it afterwards.

Well, he gave his account, and then we proceeded to the main business of the evening. The plank was set up again on the dustbins, the committee ranged themselves behind it, and the great moment was upon us. First, the members of the committee handed over to Ted the money each had collected. He called it out aloud, as he put it into the wooden box, and I wrote down the sum in my account book. Then the other members of the Combined Company filed past, one by one, each adding his or her takings. Toppy's sister, the lightning artist, had done particularly well, which proved we were right to bring girls into Operation Glazier. As the money poured in, our excited chatter died gradually down to a dazed silence. It was becoming obvious that we'd collected more money than we'd expected in our wildest dreams!

The procession ended up with a few chaps who hadn't been able to take part in any of the activities, for one reason or another, but who handed in some of their pocket money, instead. When the last chap had passed the table, and everyone was scrumming around behind, breathing down my back and trying to see the figures in the account book, I heard Toppy say, "And what about you, Prune?"

I looked up. The Prune was trying to slide away into the crowd. They pushed him out in front of the committee. The fact is that, although the Prune had agreed to come in on Operation Glazier, none of the special parties would have him at any price. Still, he could have contributed some of his pocket money, as the other boys had done.

"You've got enough money there, haven't you?" he mumbled.

"That's not the point," remarked Ted. "Everyone agreed to give something."

"Well, I've changed my mind, then."

A howl of execration rose up, and people began to advance threateningly upon the wretched Prune.

"Don't chiz!"

"Come on, Prune, fork out!

"He's a pauper!" yelled Charlie Muswell. "A stinking pauper! Spent all his pocket money on drink!"

Ted shut them up. "If he doesn't want to, he needn't. Let him go. You can buzz off, Prune," he said contemptuously.

This stung the Prune. He stepped up to the table, fairly glaring at Ted, dug his hand in his pocket and planked down half a crown.

"Fooled again," he said.

Some boys began to applaud, rather shamefacedly. After all, 2*s*.6*d*. was a good contribution.

"Thanks very much," said Ted, considerably taken aback.

"Where did you pinch it from?" asked Peter Butts.

"It's probably snide," remarked Toppy, taking up the coin, biting it, and bouncing it on the table before he threw it into the box.

"Don't be so mean, Toppy," his sister said. "It's very generous of him. He was only taking a rise out of you, pretending he wouldn't contribute."

"Yes, I fooled them all right, didn't I?" The Prune *would* go and spoil the impression he'd made, of course —gloating and showing off like that. However, nobody noticed it much, as I was beginning to add up the total in my account-book. Here it is:

	£	s.	d.
Concert Party	1	3	7½
Acrobat Troupe		12	5
Window-cleaning Detachment		8	0
Shoe-shine Detachment		7	6
Lightning Sketches: Miss E. Toppingham	1	2	0
Commission on selling Colley's Quick-Curl		5	0
Lessons in Slang		1	6
Weeding Gardens		1	0
Commission from Blind Beggar		1	0
Salary for Newspaper-round			6
Cinema Money		15	0
Private subscriptions and sale of effects at pawnbroker's		10	11½
GRAND TOTAL	5	8	6

I called out the total and a great cheer went up. We'd done it! It seemed almost impossible to believe. There was no time now to decide what should be done with the balance of the money after Nick had been given the £4 14*s.* 6*d.* for the window: so it was settled that the committee should meet at Ted's house next morning to discuss this. Ted locked the box, put the key in his pocket and the box under his arm, and set off home. The rest of us went our several ways. Peter Butts was to call in at Nick's house, and tell him to come round to Ted's at ten o'clock tomorrow.

CHAPTER V

BLACK SUNDAY

SHARP at ten o'clock on Sunday morning, I turned in at the alley which leads to Ted's back door. Otterbury is an ancient town, and there are a lot of these old-fashioned covered alleyways on the main street, leading round to the backs of the houses or shops there. Ted and his sister live in a flat above her bookshop, which of course is shut on Sundays.

Toppy and Peter Butts arrived the next minute. We were in the sitting-room, discussing what should be done with the rest of the money, after we had given Nick the amount for the window. Obviously it would have to be spent on something which all the boys and girls who had helped to collect it could share, and this made things difficult. Peter Butts suggested an outing and picnic the next day, which as you remember was our half-term holiday. But the trouble was that many of us would already be going out with our people, or have made some other plans—anyway 14*s.* would not go a long way. I was keen on starting a magazine just then, and suggested we should put the money towards buying a second-hand cyclostyling machine and form the gang into a newspaper company. However, nobody thought much of this idea. Toppy, who seemed bored with the whole business, said why not just distribute the balance of the money among the people who had collected it. At this Ted, who had been rather silent and thoughtful, said:

"I don't think we ought to use the money on ourselves at all. We raised it for charity, I mean, and it'd be like taking it under false—false——"

"False pretences?" I said.

"Yes."

"False pretences my foot!" said Peter. "We worked for it, didn't we?"

"Yes, but we weren't supposed to be working for our own benefit."

"Well, you'd better start giving back the money to the people who contributed it, then," jeered Toppy. "What a hope!"

"Ted's crazy! Give it *back*?" said Peter.

"I never said anything about giving it back. I just think we ought to give it to some charity. Why don't we ask Rickie?"

"Oh, come off it! What's it to do with him?"

I thought Ted was being rather priggish, but I felt I had to back him up.

"We might get into a row if we pocket the money," I argued. "Hundreds of people in Otterbury know about it by now. It's a sensation in the town. My mother told me everyone was talking: she said most people thought it was a jolly good show, but there were some pretty indignant about it—I mean, when they found out what N.Y.A.F. really meant. Well, these indignant folk might make things hot for us if it came out we'd spent some of the money on ourselves. But they can't object if it's given to charity."

"Oh, you're just windy," said Peter. "They can't do anything to us."

"If you think I stood up and made a fool of myself in front of half Otterbury, selling curling-tongs, just to give away the money to buy calico night-shirts for the poor benighted heathen in Africa, you've another think coming," said Toppy.

Well, there it was. We had reached a deadlock. We were still wrangling when the bell rang. It was Nick:

he explained he couldn't get here before because his aunt had given him some job to do in the house. Ted told him that the money for repairing the window had been collected all right, and you should have seen Nick's face—he looked like a criminal who has had a reprieve at the eleventh hour: it made me feel that all our planning and work had been really worth while. Ted called his sister. She came in, took a key out of a pigeon-hole in the bureau, opened one of the big drawers and put the wooden box on the table. Then Ted put his key in the lock of the box, turned it, opened the lid.

The rest of us were sitting round the table. Ted's sister had her hand on the door-knob—she's an excellent woman and never butts in where she isn't wanted.

"Come on," said Toppy, "dish it out."

Ted was standing there, staring into the box, absolutely rigid, as if it contained a nest of tarantulas or a Gorgon's head. He went white as paper, then a deep flush gradually spread all over his face. The room was suddenly dead silent; the first sound of the Abbey bells ringing up for morning service crashed into this silence like a bomb.

"What's the matter, Ted?" asked Rose Marshall.

Ted's voice was almost inaudible as he muttered, "It's not there"; but it broke the spell, and we were all crowding round him, staring into the box, then scrabbling amongst its contents—stones and old nails and screws and rusty hinges.

The money had gone. Not one halfpenny of the £5 8*s.* 6*d.* was to be found as we emptied the box on to the table and sifted through the junk.

"It's a practical joke—you're pulling our legs, Ted," I said feebly. "Aren't you?" But I somehow knew this wasn't it at all.

The money had gone

"Rose, this is the wrong box. What did you do with the one I gave you to lock up last night?" Ted asked.

"That's the box you gave me. Why, you saw me put it into the drawer yourself," she replied.

"But it's impossible. It was full of coins."

There was a bewildered silence. Then Toppy said, "Well, that solves the problem of what to do with the rest of the money."

Ted turned to Nick. "I'm awfully sorry, Nick. We had the money for you. But it's gone. I don't know what's happened."

"It's all right," replied Nick—and I must say he was taking it jolly well—" don't worry. It can't be helped."

There was another awkward pause.

"Only one thing could have happened to the money, said Toppy. "It must have been stolen."

"But that's impossible," exclaimed Rose. "I locked

it up myself, last night, and the key of the drawer was just where I left it, in this pigeon-hole."

"Well, how did all this junk get into the box, then?" asked Peter Butts.

"It's an absolute mystery."

We talked a bit more, but no one had the foggiest notion what could have happened. Well, that's not quite true. The harm had been done, of course, when Toppy said it must have been stolen. And the rest of us knew it secretly, though we didn't dare say it—knew, too, that nobody could have stolen the money except Ted or his sister.

Rose said she was going to telephone to Mr. Richards. When she left the room, Toppy said,

"We'll have to have a General Meeting about this. As soon as possible. It's serious. Come on, Peter."

"What time?" asked Ted miserably.

"We'll let you know." Toppy went to the door, then turned and added, "You'll be allowed to speak in your own defence."

Nick Yates walked right up to him and said, "If you're suggesting that Ted stole it, I'll fight you."

"Don't be an ass. Fighting won't pay for the window you broke."

"I don't care—I'll own up to my uncle about the window. But you've got no right to accuse Ted."

Nick Yates was fierce as a terrier. Talk about a snail coming out of its shell!

"We're not accusing anyone. Yet. Come on, Butts."

We heard their feet running down the stairs. Ted began to turn over the heap of junk on the table again, as though it might miraculously change back into silver and copper coins. Presently Rose came back; Rickie was with her. They both looked pretty worried.

"Well, now, there must be some simple explanation,"

Rickie began. "Just tell us everything that happened from the moment you took charge of the money yesterday evening, Ted."

Ted had come straight home, and given the box to his sister to lock up. He'd not opened the box again: the key had been in his trouser pocket all night. There wasn't a sign anywhere of the house having been broken into.

"Did you talk to anyone on your way home? Tell anyone what you had in the box?"

"No. Oh yes, I'd absolutely forgotten, sir. You know that chap, Johnny Sharp? Well, he and the man he's always about with—the Wart, we call him—they were hanging around in the alleyway below, when I got home. They asked me how much we'd collected for Nick Yates."

"What happened then?"

"Well, nothing. I told them. And Johnny Sharp took the box——"

"Oh, he did, did he?"

"No, I don't mean he stole it or anything. He just took it up in his hands, and shook it to hear the money rattle. Then he handed it to the Wart, and the Wart shook it, and gave it back to me. That's all."

"You're certain he gave you back the same box? Did you have your eye on it all the time?"

"Not absolutely all the time, sir. Because the Wart was standing behind Johnny Sharp when he rattled the box. But it was only for a moment. And—" Ted turned the box over and pointed to a cross scratched on the bottom of it—"you see that mark? I noticed it when the Prune first gave us the box. It must be the same one."

So *that* was a dead end. We talked and talked about it, but we didn't seem to get an inch further. Presently

I thought I'd better clear off. Nick came with me. We'd got to the end of the street before I realised that, in the general consternation, I'd left my cap behind. I told Nick to wait, and ran back to the Marshalls' house. The back door was not locked, so I thought I'd go quietly up the stairs and fetch the cap without disturbing anyone. But then I heard Rose Marshall's voice inside the sitting-room: she sounded angry. I couldn't help overhearing a bit of the conversation—"You might as well suspect *me* of it," she was saying.

"But, darling, who else *could* have taken it but Ted?" That was Rickie's voice, patient, kind and reasonable, like he is when he's explaining something in form to one of his less bright pupils. "After all, you've admitted it's impossible that anyone could have broken into the flat. And it *was* a temptation, for any boy, to have all that money in his charge. You must see that."

"If *you* won't believe Ted, I don't want to have anything more to do with you," said Rose wildly. "I tell you, he wouldn't do a thing like that." Her voice became sharp and cold. "Perhaps you'd like to call the police in and search the house."

I thought I'd better not listen any longer, so I charged up the rest of the stairs, making a clatter, knocked on the door, went in and found my cap. Rose and Rickie were alone in the room. They both looked pretty furious. I stood not upon the order of my going, but went. Rejoining Nick, I told him what I'd overheard. He gave me a queer look.

"D'you believe Ted took the money?" he asked point-blank.

"Well, it does look jolly suspicious, doesn't it? I mean, who else *could* have?"

"I haven't a clue. But I *know* he didn't. And, even if he did, I'd stick up for him." Nick's eyes were absolutely blazing. "What about you? What side are you on?"

"Well, naturally you stick up for him because he started the scheme for collecting the money for you, and was decent about——"

"I don't care a bit about the money. I'm going to tell my uncle now about the window, and he can do what he likes. I'm asking you, are you on Ted's side or not?"

Nick seemed to have turned into quite a different person. It was incredible. They say a crisis brings out unexpected powers in you: it certainly did with Nick Yates.

"I'll stand by Ted," I replied, feeling a bit ashamed. "But what on earth can we do?"

"Prove him innocent."

"What, just you and me? But it's——"

"You and me and anyone else who'll come in on it. There's going to be a meeting this afternoon. We'll find out then."

"But Toppy and his lot are bound to be against Ted."

"Let them. We can do without them. But if Ted's company turns against him I'll lay them out, one by one."

"A fat lot of help that'll be! Wait a minute, Nick, I've an idea. You know what Toppy's like—enthusiastic about any new craze."

"So what?"

"We'd get him interested if we made a detective job of it—sort of Murder Game. Then the rest'd come in too."

"You've got something there."

"He wouldn't do it to help Ted. But he'd do it just for the fun—bet you anything he would."

"But it isn't a game," said Nick. "It's serious."

"I know. We've got to make a game of it, though, at

first anyway, if we're to have Toppy working in with us. And we shall need everyone we can get."

By this time we had reached Nick's house. He was looking rather pale; but he took a deep breath, nodded good-bye to me, and walked stoutly in. . . .

As I walked along to the Incident that afternoon, I was pondering a thought which had occurred to me at dinner. If Ted had in fact embezzled the funds, why should he protest so vigorously that Johnny Sharp and the Wart couldn't have taken the money when they met him in the alley? Surely the natural thing, for a guilty person, is to try and fasten the guilt on someone else. Ted could easily have said they'd snatched the box from him and run off with it: it'd be his word against theirs, and they're pretty fair crooks, to look at, anyway. Then Ted could have got rid of the box somewhere and kept the money. Only a half-wit, if he'd really stolen the money, would have proceeded to fill the box with old iron and wait for it to be discovered the next day.

I put this argument at the meeting, after Ted had told his story. There were about fifteen of us there. Toppy had turned the meeting into a Court of Justice, which I thought was pretty cold-blooded of him: he was the Judge, and Peter Butts the prosecuting counsel. I said it was a farce, and the business was too serious to make a game out of it. But Toppy said it was not a game at all, as far as he was concerned, so I volunteered to be Counsel for the Defence.

My argument seemed to impress some of the Jury. I also said that, in English law, a man was held innocent until he was actually proved guilty, and the onus of proving guilt was on the Prosecution. I'd just finished my speech when Nick Yates turned up. He walked stiffly and looked very white—chastised, but not chastened, to coin an epigram. His uncle had given him a hell of a beating; and what had really upset Nick, we later discovered, he'd said he would sell Nick's puppy to help pay for the broken window.

However, Nick wasn't downhearted now. He looked round the Court and said he'd lay out anyone who believed Ted had taken the money. The Prune, who had been visibly gloating over Ted's downfall, told him he was just sucking up to Ted, and asked him to explain how the money could have disappeared if Ted hadn't swiped it. The Officers of the Court then had to restrain Nick from knocking the Prune's block off, which he showed every sign of being about to do. The proceedings looked like turning into a riot, so I got up again and asked the Judge for a remand until further evidence was collected. I said that Nick and I had the beginnings of a case against person or persons unknown.

"How can you have a case against an unknown person?" Peter Butts interrupted.

I told him this was a usual police formula, as anyone but a moron like himself would know: we were going to turn ourselves into a detective agency, I went on, and run the real criminals to earth; it was the duty of members of the general public to assist our investigations. I noticed a gleam come into Toppy's eye when I mentioned the word 'detective'. Had he taken the bait, I wondered?

Toppy—that is to say the Judge—arose. He granted a remand. Then, rather forgetting himself, he said two could play that game. All probability pointed to Ted as the culprit, and he proposed, since the Defence had challenged him to produce evidence proving Ted guilty, to do a bit of detection himself. He would be the C.I.D.;

The lost leader

and if any amateur Sherlock Holmeses cared to fool about on the other side, that was their look-out.

It was maddening. Nick and I had been hoist with our own petard. The old rivalry between Toppy and Ted had broken out again; and of course Toppy's star was in the ascendant now. Almost everyone, I could see, would join him. I shall never forget how, when Toppy proclaimed that the Court was adjourned, people stood aside and made a lane for Ted to walk through, like you do for someone to run the gauntlet; only it wasn't wet towels and such-like, it was a lane of silence and suspicion. Ted had to walk through it: the boys just drew aside from him, as if he was contaminated, and let him go. I shall never forget the look on Ted's face as he passed through this silent barrage of accusation. A line of poetry came into my head—"Just for a handful of silver he left us," and I remembered the poem is called *The Lost Leader*. And I shall never forget how Nick ran after Ted, and put his arm through Ted's and walked away with him.

CHAPTER VI

THE DETECTIVES GET TO WORK

NICK's gesture made a certain impression. Two others of Ted's old company broke away from the crowd and followed—Charlie Muswell and young Wakeley. We went to Ted's house and there we held a council of war. The worst snag was that we had so short a time to work in: there was only the rest of Sunday and the whole holiday on Monday, and then we should be back at the grindstone again. Ted said that of course he'd have to repay the money: but we knew this would mean his sister paying it, and she isn't well off; and anyway, repaying it wouldn't clear him of the guilt. But where was one to start with the investigation? The sum of £5 8*s*. 6*d*., in silver and coppers, had disappeared into thin air and been replaced by stones and scrap-iron. It was like having to investigate a miracle. We were all pretty gloomy as we sat round the table.

I tried to get a grip on myself and remember how the great detectives set to work. "Don't omit the smallest detail, however irrelevant it may seem," they always say when they are questioning witnesses. So I got Ted to repeat everything that had happened from the moment he set off home yesterday with the box until he handed it to his sister to lock up in the bureau drawer. When he got to the point where he'd been accosted by Johnny Sharp and the Wart, I stopped him.

"Describe the appearance of these individuals," I asked.

"Don't be daft; you know what they look like as

well as I do," he said with a flash of his old spirit.

"Never mind. Describe them."

So Ted started off, rather impatiently at first, but soon warming to his work. I jotted down notes, and it is partly from them that I reconstructed the description of Johnny Sharp which I have already given on page 5. Then we went on to the Wart.

"Well, he's got a round face like a bun, with two little eyes like currants stuck in it. A pasty white face. He never looks straight at you; sort of furtive expression, like a dog who knows he's done something wrong and is wondering if you know it," Ted said slowly. "He had no hat. He was wearing a scruffy old stained mackintosh and fawn-coloured flannel trousers. His shoes were dirty and down at heel, and cracked across the uppers."

Young Wakeley had begun to interrupt, but I shut him up. When Ted had finished his description, I made them re-enact the scene in the alley-way. Charlie played the part of Johnny Sharp, baring his teeth and leering at Ted in a hideous way, just like Johnny. Nick was the Wart.

"You take the box, Ted," I said—it was still lying on the sitting-room table, "go out, and come in just as you did yesterday when you entered the alley . . . O.K. Now, exactly where were these two standing?"

Ted put them in position, leaning against the wall.

"Then what happened?"

"Well, Johnny Sharp stopped me and said, 'Brought home the bacon?' "

"Did he seem to know it was money in the box?"

"Oh, yes."

"He must've guessed," put in Charlie Muswell, and told us how Sharp had warned off the oafs who were trying to molest the concert party.

We reconstructed the scene when Johnny Sharp had taken the box, shaken it, given it to the Wart to shake, then handed it back to Ted. From our reconstruction it became clear that, for a moment or two while the Wart was holding the box, Johnny Sharp had been standing between him and Ted, so that Ted did actually lose sight of the box. On the other hand, it was utterly impossible that, within this time, the Wart could have taken out the money and replaced it with scrap-iron, even if he'd had a skeleton key to unlock the box. So we were stymied once again.

I noticed young Wakeley was jigging about still, and asked him sarcastically if he wanted to leave the room.

"N-no," he stuttered eagerly. "I just w-want to know why the Wart was wearing a m-mackintosh."

"Why the blue blazes shouldn't he?" asked Charlie.

"Well, he never does. *And it was a fine day, wasn't it?*"

Talk about out of the mouths of babes and sucklings! After an instant of stunned silence, we got it; we rushed at young Wakeley and pounded him on the back.

"By gum, yes! Suppose he had another box, exactly like Ted's, and wanted to substitute it?" I said. "He'd be able to conceal it under the mackintosh."

Once again we re-enacted the episode, using a couple of large fat books instead of the real box. It worked! While Johnny Sharp held Ted in conversation, it would have been possible for the Wart, screened by Johnny, to have put the real box under his arm, beneath the mackintosh, and whipped out the fake one for Johnny to hand back! Ted remembered now that the Wart's mackintosh had been unbuttoned, which was a bit of corroborating evidence. But, the next moment, he damped our spirits down to zero again by saying:

"That's all very well. But how on earth could they

have got hold of a box exactly similar to our one—even to the cross scratched on the bottom?"

We all scratched our heads. "They must have seen our box—that's the only solution," said Nick, after a pause.

"They didn't, though," Ted answered. He went on to say that, after the Prune had presented us with the box, he'd taken it home and kept it on the chest of drawers in his bedroom until yesterday: neither Johnny Sharp nor the Wart had come into the house—he'd asked Rose about this.

"Well, I still think it's j. suspicious," said Charlie. "I mean, why did Johnny Sharp drive off the oicks who were following the concert party round? It's not the sort of thing you'd expect him to do. *Unless* he wanted us to make as much money as possible, for him to pinch later."

It was a good point, we all agreed. Then Nick exclaimed,

"I've got it! They must have broken into this house, to look for the box and take its measurements and so on."

"But how could they know about the box at all?" Ted protested. "I never told them."

"Well, the Prune might have let it out. Or anyone. I bet some of us talked about Operation Glazier beforehand, and perhaps mentioned that we had a box to keep the funds in; and you know how things get around in Otterbury," I said.

"Obviously the first thing to do is to grill the Prune," said Nick. "Find out if he told them about the box."

"A fat lot you'll get out of him!" said Charlie. "Still, it's worth trying."

"We can always beat him up," said Nick. "Third degree."

"No," I put in, "We've got to use tact. He's in with Toppy again now, and he'll have protection. Anyway, we've another thing to investigate as well. Were there any signs of your room having been feloniously entered, Ted——"

"*What* entered?"

"Bust into, then—between the time you first brought home the box and yesterday?"

"Not that I know of."

"Let's go and have a look."

We trooped upstairs to his bedroom. It's on the second floor. Obviously, unless the criminals had walked in at the back door or through the shop, and come upstairs, they must have used a ladder and got in by the bedroom window. We could see no recent scratches on the woodwork of the window, though of course the trail would have been pretty cold by now anyway. So we went down again, to interview Ted's sister. She was absolutely certain that neither Sharp nor the Wart had come to the back door last week: she admitted, looking a bit embarrassed, that Johnny Sharp was in the shop on Thursday afternoon; but she said he'd been talking to her all the time and couldn't have gone upstairs.

"Could the Wart—you know, that chap Joseph Seeds—have slipped into the shop unobserved and gone upstairs while Sharp was holding you in conversation?" I asked.

Rose admitted it was theoretically possible; but she could almost have sworn that it hadn't happened. I must say she was very decent about it all—I mean, she didn't patronise our efforts at detection as most grown-ups would have done. What's more, she gave us permission to examine the premises whenever we wished. She looked rather down-in-the-mouth, though, and I suspected this was partly the result of her quarrel with Rickie: I made a private vow to try and bring them together again when we'd cleared up the mystery of the stolen money: I suppose I've got a soft spot for Beauty in Distress.

Well, we went out into the backyard next. And here we had our first stroke of luck. I'd better describe the lay-out. The alley-way, where Ted was stopped by Sharp and the Wart, is of course at right angles to the street. It leads to an asphalt path, parallel with the street at the back of the houses. Between this path and the house-backs there are small yards: each house has one; they are separated from each other and the path by wooden fences, breast-high. Each yard has a gate leading in from the path. Up against the inside of her bit of fence, which is just about fifteen feet from the house itself, Rose Marshall had made a flower bed.

Rose borrowed a ladder for us from some neighbours, because we wanted to work out just what would happen if you tried to get in at Ted's bedroom window. We hoisted the ladder up, but the bottom end of it seemed likely to slip on the smooth surface of the yard, so we brought this end back to rest firmly in the flower bed.

We were just about to plant it there when I yelled, "Stop! Keep it off!" They thought I'd gone mad: till I pointed at two indentations in the earth of the flower bed, just where we'd have put the ladder down, and about the same distance apart as the feet of the ladder. The marks were fairly deep, and scuffed out towards the fence, as you'd expect to happen when a ladder was taken up to be carried away. Well, it never rains but it pours. Hardly had we discovered this clue when Ted gave a shout. He'd been examining the flower bed.

Just behind a clump of flowers, a few feet away from the ladder-marks, plain as a mole on a baby's bottom, there was a footprint!

It was not Ted's, or Rose's. It was much bigger—a man's footprint, without a doubt. Oh boy, oh boy, did we go up in the air! When we'd cooled down a bit, I got Ted to fetch a bucket and an empty seed-box. We placed them upside down over the footprint and the ladder-marks respectively, to ensure that these clues should not be obliterated.

What were we to do next? Nick Yates, who seemed to have turned into a sort of human bulldozer, was all for kidnapping Johnny Sharp and the Wart, dragging them along here, and fitting their feet into the print. However, saner counsels prevailed. I suggested the first thing to do was to make a plaster cast of the foot-mark—Scotland Yard always does that—and then to examine Ted's window-sill for finger-prints. Well, of course we hadn't the apparatus. Ted thought we ought to call in the regular police at this stage: but we pointed out that, if we did, the whole business would have to come out, and the police mightn't be quite so convinced of Ted's innocence as we were. Then I thought of E. Sidebotham. True, he was pretty balmy. On the other hand, as I've told you, he made a hobby of crime, and he might possibly have the necessary stuff for taking finger-prints and making a plaster cast. So it was agreed that Nick and I should interview E. Sidebotham, while Charlie, who was on better terms with Toppy than the rest of us, should make tactful inquiries whether any of his lot, particularly the Prune, had told Johnny Sharp or the Wart about the money box. Ted was to remain here and keep an eye on the flower bed. Young Wakeley had to buzz off home: but he'd certainly done his bit when he'd asked why the

Wart should have been wearing a mac on a beautiful fine day.

Nick and I rang the bell of E. Sidebotham's shop. He let us in, and took us upstairs. We told him as much of the story as we thought necessary—that a large sum of money had been stolen from Ted Marshall's room, and we had found certain clues we wanted his advice about. When I had finished my story E. Sidebotham tapped his nose with his finger, moved stealthily to the door, and flung it open, as though there might be a spy the other side. Then, carefully shutting it again, he came back and hissed right in my face.

"You suspect foul play?"

I nodded. Neither Nick nor I dared speak, lest we should burst out with the giggles we were bottling up.

"Say no more. Wait here," muttered E. Sidebotham conspiratorially, and padded out of the room.

When the door opened again, five minutes later, Nick went off with a fizzing noise, which he turned into a sort of strangled yelp like a hen with whooping-cough, and then pretended to have a severe attack of coughing. I must have been black in the face myself, trying not to laugh. For the apparition at the door was a knock-out. E. Sidebotham had put on a huge old check ulster, and a sort of Sherlock Holmes tweed hat was perched on his enormous head: what's more, he was wearing dark glasses, and a false beard which frizzed out from his chin like a sweep's brush. Seeing how we goggled at him, he said:

"Disguise is necessary for my work. You'd never have never recognised your old pal, Ernie Sidebotham, would you, boys?"

We shook our heads dumbly. We couldn't trust ourselves to speak. The great detective had not disguised his person only: he even put on a false voice—a thin, piercing falsetto which contrasted so oddly with his usual rumbling bass that Nick was pretty well in convulsions. I was filled with horror at the idea of walking through Otterbury in broad daylight with such a Guy-Fawkes-like figure. However, E. Sidebotham relieved my apprehensions by saying:

"We must not be seen together. You two go ahead. We'll meet at the premises in five minutes' time."

He was as good as his word. We showed him the ladder-marks and the footprint. He took a magnifying glass out of the satchel slung across his shoulders, went down on hands and knees, and crawled cautiously towards the footprint as though he was stalking it. He scrutinised the clues for some time, muttering to himself.

"Aren't you going to take a plaster cast?" Nick suggested.

"I've a strange feeling that I've seen this footprint before. Now whose could it have been?"

"You mean you know whose it is?" I asked excitedly.

"A long shot, Watson, a very long shot," he went on in his bloodcurdling falsetto. At that instant an idea came to me. It was a long shot, too.

"Mr. Sidebotham," I said, "you know that coat button you were examining yesterday when I came into your shop? You said you'd found it on enclosed premises. Was it here you found it?"

He reared up on hands and knees, giving me a wild sort of look from his glazed eyes. "Watson," he replied, "There are times when I have hopes of you. The answer to your query is, in one word, 'Yes.' Here. Just beside the flower bed."

He fumbled in the satchel and produced the button, then laid it on the spot where it had been found. I

Sherlock Sidebotham at work

asked him if I could borrow it. My idea was that, if we could somehow manage to compare it with the buttons on Johnny Sharp's and the Wart's coats, and discover that one of them had recently sewn on a new button, we should have yet another piece of evidence against them.

E. Sidebotham said we might borrow it. He had taken a sheet of stiff paper and a scissors from the satchel, and he was cutting the paper to the shape of the footprint. I must say he did it wizardly; the paper cut-out fitted exactly over the footprint when he'd finished. Of course the trouble was that it did not reproduce the pattern of the shoe-sole which had made it, as a plaster cast would have done. Still, it was something. And it gave Ted a bright notion. While E. Sidebotham beetled up the ladder to examine the window-sill, Ted was saying:

"Look, we can find out if Johnny Sharp or the Wart made this footprint. See how? We'll start up the Shoe-shine business again tomorrow morning."

His idea was to cut out in cardboard, using Mr. Sidebotham's paper one, a model of the footprint in the flower bed, and compare this with the soles of our two suspects. The difficulty, of course, would be to persuade them to have their shoes cleaned at all—to persuade the Wart, at any rate, whose shoes looked as if they'd never been cleaned in his life. While we were discussing this problem, the Abbey bells began to ring and Charlie Muswell had to dash off for Evensong. He'd only just gone when a voice hailed me from the other side of the fence.

"What on earth are you up to, George?"

It was Toppy, with Peter Butts. The situation, as you can imagine, called for tact. I didn't want to give away our clues to the 'regular' police: on the other hand, anything which helped to prove Ted's innocence should be made common property.

"Has Marshall any objection to our inspecting his premises?" asked Toppy in a cold, official voice.

"Have you a search warrant?" I said stiffly. It was a bit thick—the line Toppy was taking with Ted, refusing to address him directly at all.

"No," replied Toppy. "Of course, if Marshall refuses to let us come in, we shall draw our own conclusions."

"You can search the house till you're black in the face, for all I care," Ted exclaimed. He was looking white and miserable again; and I noticed Nick angrily straining at the leash. It seemed the moment for a spot of oil on the troubled waters.

"Mr. Sidebotham!" I called. "The police are here. Detective Inspector Toppingham and Detective Sergeant Butts."

He came lumbering down the ladder. "Ah, Scotland Yard," he said. "The police are baffled, eh? You should know my methods by now, Inspector. Apply them. The flower bed is not without interest."

"What on earth is he talking about?" interrupted Peter rudely.

I explained, showing them the marks in the soft soil and telling them our suspicions. Toppy shook back the lock of hair out of his eyes. He measured with a glance the ladder down which E. Sidebotham had just climbed. Then he turned to Ted.

"What time do you normally go to bed?"

"About nine o'clock. Why?"

"Never mind why. Did you go to bed later than this any night last week?"

"I—no, I don't think so."

"Do you sleep soundly?"

"I suppose so. But what——?"

"So soundly that you wouldn't have been woken up if someone had entered your bedroom by that window?"

"Well, no. I expect it would have woken me."

Ted had said it before I could stop him. It was a most damaging admission. I could see now what Toppy's questions were leading to. Toppy went on remorselessly:

"You're suggesting, then, that someone came into the yard, *in broad daylight*, with a ladder the length of this one, and climbed up, and got through your window, to look at the box, and none of the neighbours noticed anything queer about it?"

"He probably pretended to be a house-painter, or a window-cleaner," said Nick. "That's what thieves often do."

"Everyone in Otterbury knows Johnny Sharp and the Wart, and knows that neither of them ever does a stroke of work. It'd have been all over the town if they'd started cleaning windows. Anyway, your sister would have seen them."

"Not if she was in the shop," replied Ted.

"Yes, and on Thursday afternoon Ted's sister says Johnny Sharp came into the shop and kept her talking a long time," I put in excitedly. "The Wart could have brought the ladder round and done the job while his accomplice was holding her in conversation."

"Oh, could he just? Let's try. The Wart is a puny specimen, and Mr. Sidebotham—beg his pardon, Mr. Sherlock Holmes—is a big, strong chap. Would you mind lifting the ladder down, and then putting it up to the window again?"

Well, that tore it. E. Sidebotham got the ladder down, with some difficulty: but, try as he would, he

Our theory collapses

couldn't lift the heavy thing up again. It's a knack, I dare say. It ought to have been very funny, seeing him in his false beard and absurd tweed hat, puffing and blowing with the strain of the ladder: but nobody even smiled. I think it was then that I first realised how serious the whole business was.

"Well, how do you explain those marks in the flower bed?" I asked Toppy.

"It's not for *me* to explain them. But maybe Marshall made them himself, to divert suspicion."

This was too much for Ted. He rushed blindly at Toppy, and in doing so cannoned against E. Sidebotham who was still struggling with the ladder. The man was taken off balance, let the ladder go with a crash, and reeling backwards tripped over it and fell down near the flower bed. Even then, nobody laughed. Ted and I went to help him up. As we did so, he said a very curious thing.

"That's the second time this has happened."

He looked at us in a dazed sort of way, then put his hand to his face, felt the false beard, unhooked it, stuffed it in his pocket and shambled away out of the yard.

"Come on, Butts," said Toppy. "We needn't waste any more time here. It's quite obvious *it was an inside job*."

CHAPTER VII

THE CLUE OF THE BITTEN HALF-CROWN

BETIMES the next morning, Ted and I set up the Shoe-shine stall again by the traffic-lights in West Street. Charlie Muswell and Nick were to work the Flit gun from the basement of Rose Marshall's shop. But how different it all was from the high hopes and high spirits of Saturday morning! Even the sky looked different—one of those grey, close, dull summer skies that shuts you in like an enormous dish-cover. I remember I had a queer feeling of gloom: not depression exactly, but a feeling that it was all make-believe, that our theories and detection were just a feeble playing at something which wasn't a game at all: so why bother to go on with them. Ted hardly spoke a word for some time. He didn't seem able to keep his mind on the job, even. When at last a man asked to have his shoes cleaned, Ted started off vigorously enough, but then the brush moved slower and slower till it stopped, and Ted was staring at nothing, the brush poised in the air, and I had to take it out of his hand and finish the job.

Well, the morning wore on, and still there was no sign of Johnny Sharp or the Wart. Finally I told Ted he must go and look for them.

"Tell them their shoes need cleaning?" he said gloomily. "How on earth can I do that?"

"Brace up! Get them along here on some pretext. Tell Johnny Sharp your sister wants to see him."

"But she loathes the sight of him."

"He's far too conceited to realise that. Go on, you've got to do something."

"I don't know where they live."

That was a snag, of course. In real life, the police always know where to lay their hands on a member of the criminal classes whom they want to pull in. It made things seem more futile and make-believe than ever. However, I braced up my morale, and told Ted to try around Skinner's yard first, as they were so often hanging about there. He went slowly off, as if all the cares of the world were weighing on him. It was terrible to see so bright and resourceful a chap as Ted brought down to this. I felt myself smouldering with rage against whoever it was that had taken the money and left Ted to bear the blame. Things seemed to have reached rock bottom, but worse was to come.

A few minutes after Ted had left, Toppy and Peter Butts rolled up. Toppy was pushing the wooden hand-cart which E. Sidebotham uses for delivering his papers.

"We're just trying an experiment," he said in a sinister way, and they disappeared into the alley. When they emerged again, they were looking as smug as sin.

"Poor old Sherlock Holmes!" said Peter Butts.

"The clue of the detective's footprint!" said Toppy: and they both burst into roars of laughter. I asked them what on earth they meant. They were only too delighted to tell me. The evening before, Toppy had been struck by E. Sidebotham's curious remark, "That's the second time this has happened." It was reasonable to suppose that the man referred to his falling down in the Marshalls' back yard. From this, Toppy had deduced that it must have happened when he was delivering papers, as he wouldn't be there for any other purpose. This gave Toppy the idea which was to wreck my whole theory. He had gone round to see E. Sidebotham earlier this morning, and borrowed the handcart. And now he had just discovered that the marks in the flower bed, which I'd said were made by the ends of a ladder, perfectly fitted the two legs of this handcart. What was still worse, Toppy had borrowed one of E. Sidebotham's boots, and this boot fitted exactly into the mysterious footprint.

Obviously what had happened was that the man had tripped when coming into the Marshalls' yard, made the footprint and driven the handcart's legs deep into the soil in falling or in pulling himself to his feet again. And no doubt the button he had found on 'enclosed premises' was his own, torn off his coat somehow in the process—probably it had got caught on the handcart when he fell. There's no doubt that E. Sidebotham is a mild case of dual personality—you know, the Jekyll & Hyde thing. A shock, like falling down, switches him from Sidebotham to Sherlock Holmes, or vice versa, as we'd seen yesterday evening. When he was his Sherlock self, he could remember nothing about his ordinary self. And yesterday he'd been detecting his own 'crime.'

Toppy and Peter rubbed it in, as you can imagine. I said that at any rate it proved Ted hadn't made the marks himself, as Toppy had suggested, to divert suspicion.

"No. It just means you're back where you started, with Ted Marshall as the only possible suspect," said Toppy. "Well, talk of the devil——!"

He pointed up the street, and I saw Ted coming along with Johnny Sharp and the Wart. As they came up, Johnny flopped his hand at us and bared his teeth in a foxy smile. Ted got them standing in front of the basement grating for a few moments, while he pretended to show them a book in the shop-window. From sheer force of habit, I called out "Shoe-shine, threepence!" Johnny Sharp, who was cocking his hat at his reflection in the window, looked down at his feet. Then he gave us a nasty leer.

"Coo, what a racket!" he exclaimed. "Think this up yourselves? You ought to be in Big Business, like me, not this small-time stuff. O.K., I'll buy it." And he put his foot on the shoe-shine stand.

I knelt down and set to work with the brushes. Ted was beside me, breathing excitedly, looking to see if Sharp's foot fitted the cardboard cut-out we'd fixed on the stand with drawing-pins. Naturally, I hadn't had time to tell Ted the truth about the footmark, so he was all agog. Anyway, Johnny Sharp's foot was much smaller than the cut-out, and a different shape—he had ghastly, spivvish shoes, with pointed toes.

When I'd finished them, he called to the Wart. "Come on, Jose! Frippence-worth for you. Might as well try and look like a gent when you go around with me. And you can pay for mine too, seeing as you're in the money."

He pranced off into the shop, swinging his padded shoulders. The Wart put his shoe on the stand. And what a shoe! Patent leather gone to seed. Poor old Ted's face was a study. Of course the Wart's foot didn't fit the cut-out either. Toppy and Peter Butts were grinning away like Cheshire cats in the background. And Ted was on hot bricks now, because at any moment Johnny Sharp might come whizzing out of the shop to inquire just what Ted had meant by telling him his sister wanted to see him.

The Wart put half a crown in the saucer, to pay for Johnny and himself. We hadn't got enough change, so I popped into the shop to get some from Rose. Johnny Sharp must have left the door ajar, for the bell did not ring when I went in. He was saying to Rose,

"What's the idea, sending for me, then? What d'you want?"

I sidled quietly behind a book-case.

"There's only one thing I want," Rose Marshall replied.

"Name it, ducks, and you shall have it."

"I want you to get out of my shop, this minute."

"Now don't go all Roedean with me, beautiful. I reckon I can do you a bit of good." Johnny Sharp leant over the counter and began talking out of the side of his mouth. "That kid-brother of yours. In trouble, ain't he?"

"How do *you* know he's——"

"I get around, baby. Suppose the flatfeet got to hear of it? Sticky look-out for young Ted, eh? Disgrace on the dear old family name. And what's *Mister* Richards doing about it?"

"Get out, you overdressed, crawling louse!" said Rose, in a voice like rusty barbed-wire.

"Overdressed?" Johnny Sharp sounded quite stung for once. "And me paying twenty smackers for this suit? Genuine Savile Row." He flapped his hand at her. "Nah. Come off it. I can do you a bit of good over young Ted. If you'll be nice to me. Just a little kiss, to be going on with."

I thought it was time to make my presence felt, so I banged the door behind me as if I'd just come in, and asked for change of half a crown.

The chaps at school once used to call me Professor, because I was so absent-minded. Well, it turned out a mercy I'd been absent-minded again and forgotten to take the half-crown out of the saucer. Rose gave me the change. I popped out again and handed the Wart 2*s*. He slouched off to lean against a lamp post till Johnny Sharp came out: the Wart always had to prop himself

Johnny Sharp is called a louse

up against something. Toppy took the half-crown and began to spin it.

"Heads I win, tails you lose. Call!"

"Shut up, Toppy, I've got to give it to Ted's sister."

He had caught the coin on the back of his left hand and smacked his right palm over it. He was in one of his obnoxious teasing moods; I knew from bitter experience the fatal thing would be to lose my temper or try to snatch it from him. So I just stood and waited. Johnny Sharp emerged from the shop and walked away with the Wart. Ted, who had been hiding in the alley, came out.

"Hand it over, Toppy," he said, "it belongs to my sister."

"Not to the Nick Yates Assistance Fund?" asked Peter Butts nastily. "What's up, Toppy?"

Toppy was staring at the back of his hand, as if a plague spot had suddenly appeared on it. It gave me quite a turn. After a moment or two of absolute silence, he walked up to Ted, put out his right hand, and said:

"I'm sorry. I was wrong about you taking the money. I know now that you didn't. Put it there."

"What on earth——?"

Toppy always liked to do things the most dramatic way. And he certainly had an audience now.

"I have here a clue to the mystery. A simple, ordinary coin of the realm, vulgarly known as half a crack or a demi-dollar. A less brilliant and alert investigator than myself——." He couldn't keep it up any longer— "Look, chaps, teeth-marks! *My* teeth-marks!"

We were crowding round him, still absolutely in the dark. He went on, his eyes blazing at our mystified faces.

"Don't you remember? The half-crown the Prune subscribed? I fastened my fangs in it and bounced it on the table, and said it was probably snide. This is the very one. It can't be a coincidence. I remember my teeth made these marks right across the King's head on it."

"*Gosh!*" I exclaimed. "And the Wart has just put it in the saucer. Which means it *was* he who stole the money."

"You're coming on, Holmes."

"I don't see that it follows," said Peter Butts stubbornly. "Ted could have bought something with it at a shop, and then the Wart might have gone to the same shop later and got it as change."

It was my turn to crow. "Oh, jolly bright!" I said. "Only, as it happens, the shops were shut before Ted took the money box home on Saturday, and they're all shut on Sunday, and I've been with Ted this morning since before they opened. Anyone but a half-wit would have seen all that."

Peter Butts had to admit that Ted's innocence was proved. We fetched Nick and Charlie out of the basement, told Rose what had happened, then went up to Ted's room for a council of war.

Ted was in favour of going straight to the police with the bitten half-crown. But Peter pointed out that this wouldn't get Nick Yates' money back.

"They've probably spent it, anyway," said Charlie Muswell.

"That's the whole point," I said. "The police can't compel them to disgorge their ill-gotten gains. But we can make them pay the money back by threatening to go to the police with our story."

"They'd just call our bluff," Toppy put in. "We haven't enough proof yet."

Nick was up in arms at once. "Not enough proof? You mean you still think Ted *may* have taken it?"

"Kindly do me the favour of dropping down dead," Toppy replied good-humouredly. "*I* know Ted didn't take it. But we haven't enough evidence to prove that Johnny Sharp and the Wart *did*."

"And we never will, unless we find out how they managed to switch the two boxes," said Charlie.

We all stared at one another despondently, chewing the toffee Ted had very decently provided out of his sweet ration. It seemed a hopeless nut to crack.

"Look here," I suggested at last, "let's try to work it out another way. Put ourselves in the place of the criminals. Toppy, suppose you were Johnny Sharp——"

"Thanks awfully."

"—and you wanted to get hold of our wooden money box, to make a replica of it."

"I wouldn't climb into Ted's room in broad daylight, I can tell you that."

"Well, what follows?"

"Search me."

Nick suddenly gave a yell, which so startled me that I half swallowed my toffee and nearly choked to death.

"I've got it!" he shouted, snapping his fingers. "*He must have known about the box already!*"

"What is this, Yates? Explain yourself," said Toppy in the Headmaster's chilly tones.

"If Johnny Sharp couldn't have seen the box *after* the Prune gave it to Ted, he must have seen it *before*. That's logic."

"It's plumb crazy to me," said Peter Butts. "How could he?"

But Toppy was looking as excited as Nick now. "You're right. He could have given it to the Prune himself, to pass on to us."

It was so easy. Everything fell into place. The Prune had walked away from the original meeting when it was decided to raise funds for Nick, refusing to take part. But later he had come back with the box. Why had he changed his mind, and where had he got the box? According to the theory we worked out between us, Prune must have met Johnny Sharp and the Wart, mentioned to them what we were planning: the two criminals saw an opportunity for easy money, and told the Prune to give us the box without saying where it came from—bribed him, maybe, for it wasn't very likely that the Prune could have afforded otherwise the 2*s*.6*d*. he later subscribed. Johnny Sharp either possessed a duplicate box, or made one between then and Saturday.

"How can we prove all this?" asked Ted.

"Easy. We'll put the Prune to the question," answered Toppy with a sinister glance.

"Yeah. Third-degree him," said Nick.

"Skin him alive and hang him up to dry," said Charlie Muswell.

We all tore downstairs and pelted along to the Prune's house. He wasn't in, but his father said he'd gone down to the river to fish.

The Biddle is a fair-sized river, about seventy yards at its broadest where the road bridge spans it on the outskirts of Otterbury. A bit further west there is a place where you can hire boats, and beyond that a bathing pool. When we got to the bridge, we looked up and down the river. In the distance, downstream, just about where the allotments and shacks peter out into meadowland along the south bank, we spotted a bright-yellow object. It was one of those ex-R.A.F. dinghies which the boatman lets out cheap. A figure with a rod sat motionless in it.

"There he is!" shouted Nick and started haring off the bridge towards the towing-path. Toppy caught him up, and stopped him.

"Don't be a fool! He'll take fright if he sees a whole army charging down at him. Leave it to me."

The rest of us were to approach the objective by a detour through the town, while Toppy and Peter sauntered towards it along the towing-path.

Five minutes later, as we crept through the allotments towards the water's edge, I heard Toppy hail the doomed Prune. We took cover behind a shack, some thirty yards away, and I pulled out my notebook to write

The Prune about to be grilled

down the evidence. Round the corner of the shack we could see the Prune very slowly take in his line, lay down the rod, put on the paddle-gloves, and propel the inflated dinghy towards the shore. Ted was stiff as a statue, Nick quivering with impatience like a terrier at a rat-hole. I was feeling pretty strung up myself. We had about twelve hours to solve the mystery, unless we cut school tomorrow. Knowing it was a race against time, and the Prune was only the first hurdle to be jumped, made everything seem to go in slow-motion. The white paddle-gloves dipped so slowly into the water, the dinghy yawed sluggishly from side to side; twice the Prune stopped altogether and asked Toppy what on earth he wanted, interrupting his fishing.

Finally he reached the bank and scrambled ashore.

Toppy was sitting on the bank, kicking his heels, just as if nothing was up at all. He said:

"We've got a message for you. From a friend of yours."

"What friend?"

"Johnny Sharp."

I could see the Prune go tense. He gave a half-look behind him, as if he might jump back into the dinghy; but Peter Butts, reaching out his foot, had pushed it away from the bank.

"Johnny Sharp? I hardly know him. What the——?"

"Johnny Sharp wants you to tell us all about the box he lent you—the one you gave Ted to keep the money in."

Ted's name was the prearranged signal for the rest of us to come out of hiding. The Prune looked round wildly, but we and the river hemmed him in on all sides.

"I don't know what you're talking about."

"You'd better come clean, and double quick. We know he gave you the box, and——"

"Well, what if he did?"

"Ah, you admit that. Tell us just what happened, and we'll leave you alone."

"And if I don't——?"

"We'll put you in the river and hold your head under water till you do talk."

"How can I talk with my head under water?"

"Don't try to be funny. It doesn't suit you. . . . Well? . . . We'll give you five seconds to open your stinking mouth. Five. Four. Three. Two. One——GET HIM!" Toppy hurled himself at the Prune, knocked him over and sat on his chest. "Ted, gag him with your handkerchief. The rest of you, tie up his arms and legs."

Toppy very deliberately looked at his watch and said, "The *first* time we'll only hold you under water for twenty seconds. The next time it will be thirty. After that——"

But the Prune, by frantic gestures, made it clear that his nerve had cracked. We unstoppered him, and the story poured out.

CHAPTER VIII

SHADOWS AND SHOCKS

OUR deductions had been correct. The Prune had met Johnny Sharp and the Wart that day as he sloped off from our meeting, and told them what we were planning. According to his story, Johnny Sharp had been very interested: he took the Wart aside a moment, and muttered something in his ear, which the Prune thought was "Skinner's workshop." The Wart went off into Skinner's yard—I suppose we were all too excited planning Operation Glazier to notice him—and presently returned with a wooden box, which Johnny Sharp gave the Prune to pass on to us: he also gave him five bob to keep his mouth shut, telling him he must on no account let us know where the box came from. Closely cross-questioned, the Prune denied that he had suspected anything fishy about all this, though I'd bet a 5-lb. iced cake against a stale rock-bun that he had a pretty good idea what was going on, if indeed he wasn't in the plot as an accomplice, because he'd certainly have done anything to get even with Ted after Ted had knocked his block off during the tank ambush.

Anyway, Toppy told him we'd cut his throat if he breathed a word to Johnny Sharp or the Wart about his confession—not that he'd be likely to—and gave him a boot which lifted him well into the middle distance. Then we retired into the shack for a conference. The atmosphere (which was compounded of the smells of creosote and bone manure, incidentally) fairly buzzed with bright ideas. I won't relate them all—only the ones we finally adopted. Viz.:

(i) to send out the fiery cross and summon all of Ted's and Toppy's companies who weren't away for the day with their parents. Rendezvous, the Incident: time 14.15 hours.

(ii) to shadow the criminals for the rest of the afternoon, and if possible to drive a wedge between them, metaphorically speaking; the Wart was obviously the soft underbelly of their Axis, and we might be able to break his nerve somehow if we could detach him from Johnny Sharp.

(iii) —hold everything now, this is the big bang coming—to get into Skinner's workshop! From the revolting Prune's evidence, it was clear that the original box had come from there. So, we argued, there was every likelihood that the duplicate one also had; and that the criminals had brought back the original box there, after getting it off Ted, to open it and share out the cash. We might find evidence of the boxes having been made in Skinner's workshop. We might even find the first box still there, because Johnny Sharp and the Wart wouldn't have been likely to take such an incriminating object back to their own homes, which might well have been searched by the police if Ted had told them about his meeting with the criminals in the alley. On the other hand, they could feel pretty safe at the workshop, since Johnny had gone out of his way to conceal his connection with Skinner.

It was vital that we should try to recover the original box, for it would be a conclusive piece of evidence against Johnny Sharp and the Wart. Without it, our case might fall to the ground. But to break into Skinner's workshop was a difficult and dangerous project. All of us in the shack volunteered, of course. But I must say I was j. relieved, being an historian rather than a man of action, when Ted and Toppy said they would form the Commando unit for this operation themselves, just the pair of them.

They would certainly make a good team. Toppy has the dare-devil spirit more than anyone I know, and he could bluff his way out of an alligator's jaws: Ted is slower, but more obstinate and reliable. If Toppy is tops at spur-of-the-moment tactics, Ted is a born strategist. This had come out at the ambush in Abbey Lane; and it came out again now. It was he who worked out in detail the plans for shadowing and separating the two criminals, and for getting into Skinner's place: he seemed to think of everything, including the pieces of chalk and the bogus telephone call—but read on and you'll see what I mean by these cryptic remarks.

To go back for a moment. A detective must show that his suspect has had (a) means, (b) opportunity, (c) motive for the crime. Our suspects had certainly had the opportunity. If we found the box it would prove they had had the means, though the bitten half-crown and the fact of Johnny Sharp's presenting the original box would probably be enough to convince most juries. The only snag was the motive. Why should a chap like Johnny Sharp, who flashed wads of notes in one's face, go to such trouble to pinch a few pounds from a gang of 'kids'? Somehow it didn't ring true to me. Peter Butts, who is a cynical type, said that if you were a natural crook like Sharp you'd bump off your grandmother for 6*d.*: big money, small cash, it didn't matter, it was all grist to your mill. Well, honestly I don't believe it.

Anyway, as we walked back into the town, I was revolving in my mind all that I knew of the criminal mentality—which, I admit, comes chiefly from books, though Mr. Robertson did say once that for a Rogue's Gallery and Chamber of Horrors rolled into one, nobody need go further than the Upper Fourth at our school. Vanity is supposed to be a chief characteristic of the criminal. Now there's no doubt that Johnny Sharp is vain: and it occurred to me, he may really be vain enough to believe that Rose Marshall would marry him: he always seems to be pestering her, anyway. Perhaps, in his warped mind, he had thought that, if he could get Ted into trouble with the police and then somehow save him—for instance by owning up to having taken the money himself and pretending it had been a practical joke—Ted's sister would be grateful and look more favourably upon his advances. It sounds pretty childish, written down like this, I know: but the criminal, I read in one of my father's books, often has a strong streak of infantilism. Certainly what I'd heard Johnny Sharp say to Rose in the shop this morning did seem to bear out this theory. . . .

Well, between the five of us, we managed to collect over a dozen of the two companies, and we left urgent messages for the rest to join us when they got home. At 14.15 we made our rendezvous. Ted outlined the plans for the shadowing, and everyone was pretty enthusiastic. While our meeting was still on, the double doors of Skinner's yard were opened and Skinner himself drove out in a lorry. It seemed a good opportunity for getting into his workshop; but Ted and Toppy decided not to alter their plans for the Commando raid, which had been timed to take place later in the afternoon. As it turned out, if they *had* changed their plans, they would have escaped a hair-raising ordeal, but also they would have missed making the discovery which was to reverberate through Otterbury like a thunderclap.

Shortly after Skinner's departure, Charlie Muswell came tearing up. He and Nick had been detailed to watch the Crooked Man, a pub near the station where Johnny Sharp and the Wart were often to be found at dinner-time. Charlie reported that the enemy had been observed drinking in the pub, and Nick was shadowing them. We all raced off in great spirits. It was a bit of luck, making contact with the enemy so quickly. But, when we got to the Crooked Man, the doors were shut and nobody in sight. It was after closing time.

"Where's Nick? Have they kidnapped him, d'you think?" somebody asked.

"Don't be an ass," Ted replied. "Cast about for chalk marks."

It was here that Ted's forethought proved its value. He had arranged for everyone to carry a piece of chalk, so that if the main body lost touch with any of their scouts, they could pick up the trail through chalk-marks. Presently young Wakeley gave a yell. He had found two arrows in chalk on a pillar box near-by, pointing towards the station. Ted spat on his handkerchief and rubbed them out: it might be confusing if the enemy came back this way before we caught up with them, and Nick had to make more chalk-marks to guide us. Two arrows, by the way, meant that our quarry were still together.

We hurried along towards the station, finding another pair of arrows on a wall in Station Road, and then a third on the pavement pointing straight at the level crossing. Here we had our first check, for the gates were shut, and it would have been suicide to go through the small pedestrian's gate at the side, with the

Devon Belle bearing down a hundred yards away at about 80 m.p.h. We waited, straining at the leash, while the West-country class engine bellowed past, its crack train of pullmans swaying behind it like a comet's tail, and the passengers gazing peacefully out from the glass observation car at the end, like fish in an aquarium. Then we rushed across through the side-gates. We spread out over the goods yard on the far side, looking for the next chalk mark. It was like looking for a nigger in a dark cellar, or an albino on a snowfield if you like, because so many of the trucks had chalk writing on their sides.

At last I discovered Nick's arrows, on the side of a warehouse, pointing along the road which leads back over a railway bridge into the centre of the town. Off we dashed, picking up the trail of arrows more easily now, till they brought us to E. Sidebotham's shop. And here, on a wooden board used for displaying posters, we saw Nick's mark again: but this time it was a single arrow, with a W at the end, and very faint. The enemy had separated. The sign indicated the direction in which the Wart had gone. So far, so good. But our hearts sank when it became painfully apparent that the arrow trail had petered out. We went a hundred yards down this street, but there were no more of them to be found.

"What on earth is Nick playing at?" Peter Butts asked.

"Chalk run out, I expect. The last mark was pretty faint."

This, we discovered later, was exactly what had happened. We were baffled. But Nick had acted in a resourceful way. Toppy had the bright notion of going into E. Sidebotham's shop and asking if Nick had left any message for us.

"He said to tell you to look on the windows."

"Look on the windows? Is that all he said?"

"Well, young gents, that was all the message. After he'd asked me to oblige him with a strip of sticky paper."

Toppy let out a whoop. We tore down the street in his wake; and there, sure enough, fifty yards down, stuck on the bottom left-hand corner of a ground-floor window, was a strip of paper with an arrow pencilled on it. As we gathered round, sixteen or seventeen of us, the muslin curtains parted and an old dame was peering out at us, her jaws chumbling away silently as if she was chewing the cud. Toppy politely took off an imaginary hat, and said:

"Forgive the intrusion, Madam, I had no idea this was the camel house."

Of course she couldn't hear what he said, the window being shut. But she did look so like a camel, we yelled with laughter. Then off down the street again, following the trail quite easily now, till we came to a cross-road; and there, on the window of a scrubby little cobbler's shop, we found the message "Heading for Recreation Ground."

The Recreation Ground was a few hundred yards away, over the cross-roads. When we got there, we found Nick at the gate. He pointed. The Wart was sitting on a bench, watching some kids playing on the swings.

"Well done, Nick. Jolly good show," said Ted.

"Now what do we do?" Peter Butts asked.

Speaking for myself, this simple remark came like a bucket of iced water poured over a sleepwalker's head. A shock, a horrible chill, a feeling of what on earth am I doing here. You see, up to this point, our tracking had been a game, a sort of dream really: but now the trail had led us up to the edge of reality, up to a precipice with the quarry in view on a ledge half-way down, so to speak. And it wasn't a game or a dream any longer. I felt empty and vague; a sense of anticlimax oppressed me. That comes of being an imaginative type, I suppose. Nick had no doubts.

"Go in and scrag him," he said.

"Sit on his head and tear his bags off," said Charlie Muswell.

"No," Ted replied firmly. "This is where the war of nerves begins." He gave us certain instructions. Then we trooped into the Recreation Ground, walked over to the bench where the Wart was sitting, and sat down on the grass in a semi-circle, facing him. We said nothing at all. We just sat there, all of us staring at him. His eyes slithered round the semi-circle.

"Hello, you kids," he said.

We stayed dead silent, dead still.

"Well, what d'you want?"

Not a word or a movement from the semi-circle of watchers.

The Wart passed his tongue over his lips.

"Well, clear off, then!"

He half rose, in a menacing way. Each of us half rose too. His eyes slithered over our heads, as if looking for help. He shrugged his shoulders, slumped back on the bench, and lit a cigarette. His fingers were shaking a bit, I noticed. We all sat down again.

"Come on, chums. What's all this about? Got nothing better to do? Why not have a go on the swings?" he asked with a sickly smile.

We said nothing. We just went on looking at him.

Twice more he rose, as if to break through the cor-

The war of nerves

don; then sat down again and pretended to ignore us. Minutes passed slowly as hours. The kids who had been playing on the swings gathered curiously round and added their stares to ours, gazing at the Wart as if he were a monstrosity or a leper.

At last, Ted made a slight sign. Toppy came out of the semi-circle and sat down facing us, his back turned to the Wart.

"I'll tell you a story," he said. "Once upon a time a boy broke a window——"

And he related all the events of the last week, how we collected the money, how Ted was met by two men (he did not mention their names) in the alley-way, how the boxes were changed, how the bitten half-crown turned up again, and so on. It was like Counsel for the Prosecution making his speech. All the time he was speaking, we continued to gaze, not at him, but at the Wart. And if ever there was discomfiture and guilt in a man's face, I saw it in the Wart's then. His cigarette went out. His fingers flickered nervously, like his eyes. He mopped his brow. At one point he muttered something to himself.

When Toppy had finished, he came back and joined the semi-circle again. The Wart made one more attempt.

"You making all this up?" he said. "Why don't you go to the police about it, chums, if it's true?"

Silence.

Another ten minutes passed. Then Toppy rose, came out in front of us, sat down and said:

"I'll tell you a story. Once upon a time a boy broke a window. He——"

It was too much for the Wart. Like the window, his nerve broke. He swore a frightful oath, flung down his unlit cigarette, and plunged through the semi-circle. Nobody tried to stop him. We just got up and followed him in a mass, out of the Recreation Ground, up the street towards the Abbey, about ten paces behind, still not saying a word. Once or twice he looked round, then quickened his pace, then walked slower again as if he was trying to pretend to himself that he was just sauntering through the town in the normal way of business.

As we approached the traffic lights in West Street, we saw a policeman ahead. Toppy's genius for tactics now came out again. He ran ahead, past the Wart, and spoke to the policeman. He was, in fact, only asking him the time. But the Wart was not to know this. Seeing Toppy go up to the policeman, he stopped dead in his tracks, turned, and dashed back through our midst, bowling young Wakeley over into the gutter.

We pursued him down the street. He ran in a queer, wobbling way, with his heels and elbows flying out wide: but fear lent him wings, and he would have outdistanced us if people in the street had not got in his way. Of course, none of them was sure if he ought to be stopped or not, as we didn't want to raise a hue and cry yet. He dashed round a corner, over the Abbey Green; glanced round, saw us converging upon him from either side, and slipped in through the west door of the Abbey.

Ted called a halt. He consulted rapidly with Charlie Muswell who, being in the choir, was familiar with the terrain. Then he directed six of us, in pairs, to watch this west door and the two smaller ones, which face the Abbey Green, with instructions to blow their whistles if the Wart slipped out again while we were searching for him inside, and to follow him. There is only one door on the other side of the Abbey, and this is the Vestry door, which Charlie assured us was always kept locked—only the clergy, choirmaster and vergers having keys to it.

The rest of us now filed into the Abbey. I don't know about the others; but my own eyes turned automatically towards the altar, expecting to see the Wart clutching it, as in the olden days fugitives from justice did when they sought sanctuary. But there was no figure cowering by the great high altar, no figure at the altar of either of the side chapels; nowhere in the vast building, lit by sun-shafts which struck through the stained-glass windows and poured patches of blue and green and blood-ruby on the stone floor of the aisles, was the fugitive to be seen.

We searched all over the building. The nave, the chapels, the choir; behind the altar; in the bell-ringers' place and up in the organ loft. We searched the cupboards in the Vestry. We even split up and looked under the seats of all the pews in the side aisles (the main aisles have chairs instead of pews, so it didn't take long to assure ourselves he was not there).

Joseph Seeds, alias the Wart, had disappeared into thin air. We collected again near the west door, gazing at each other in wild surmise.

"Perhaps he's been taken up to heaven in a fiery chariot," said young Wakeley.

"What a hope!" said Peter Butts. "More likely gone below. Down amongst the devils and the toasting-forks."

"Taken up to heaven! Oh lord, I quite forgot!" Charlie Muswell exclaimed. "The Abbey tower! He must have fled up there."

We followed him into the bell-ringers' chamber again; and there, behind a curtain, he revealed a small door set in the stone wall. The door was ajar!

You may be surprised that nobody had thought of this before. But there is a strict rule at our school against going up the Abbey tower, in case some nitwit should take it into his head to jump off or to drop heavy objects on the heads of people below, I suppose. And it so happened that none of those present had ever felt an urge to break this particular rule.

At this point Ted made a false move, though I must say he can hardly be blamed, since Toppy persuaded him into it.

"Call in the sentries," Toppy said. "Let's all go up after him."

Ted looked a bit dubious about this. But Charlie Muswell said the Wart obviously must have gone up to the tower, and he couldn't get down again past us on the narrow spiral staircase. And Toppy emphasised the importance of numbers, for their psychological effect on the Wart. So Ted gave way, the sentries outside the Abbey were called in, and we all began to make our way, a chain of boys like some giant centipede, slowly creeping up the winding stairway. Ted was leading, then came Toppy, Peter Butts and myself.

After climbing what seemed like three miles of steps, round and round and round, I felt as dizzy as if I'd been on a roundabout at a fair. The leaders paused for breath on a sort of gallery overlooking the belfry. I'd no idea the bells would be so huge. They were like buoys at sea, and I could imagine them tumbling and rocking when the ropes were pulled. Just at that moment, there came a deafening clash, which made my heart stop dead. It was the chimes striking for four o'clock. As if it was a signal, reminding us that we only had a few hours left to wring a confession from the criminals, to get our money back and pay for the window and save Nick from having his puppy sold by that stinking guardian of his, we moved off again, faster now, running up the stone stairs, bumping against the walls, brushing through cobwebs, our feet clattering like hammers.

Then we were at the top. A stone landing and a wooden door. Ted turned the handle, pushed. The door opened a little, then slammed shut again. All the boys, pushing up from behind us, forced it gradually back. It gave way suddenly. Ted and Toppy were hurled through it and went sprawling across the leaden floor of the tower. Close behind them, I came out into the open air. When my eyes had stopped dazzling with the sunlight, I saw the Wart, his face sickly white as a slab of half-cooked veal, pressing himself back against the coping in the far corner of the tower.

Now we had him! He'd come to the end of his tether

all right. For the last time we formed our semi-circle, cutting him off from the door. For the last time, Toppy began:

"I'll tell you a story. Once upon a time there was——"

"Ow, cheese it," interrupted the Wart. "What d'you little twerps want?"

"We want our money back."

"What money?"

"You know very well."

"On my ruddy oath, I don't——"

"Charlie, go and fetch that policeman who's waiting," snapped Toppy. The bluff worked. We helped it by narrowing our semi-circle round the Wart, who gave one glance over the coping: the ground was very far below.

"Yurr, wait a minute. You don't want to go dragging the cops in. It was only a game, see? A joke, like."

"O.K. Well, the game's over now. Shell out," said Toppy.

"But I haven't got it. Me and Johnny shared out, see? And I bin and spent a bit of it."

"You'll have to get the money for us, then. We'll give you till six o'clock," said Ted.

A look of stupid cunning flickered over the Wart's face.

"Sure, I'll get it for you. Five pounds odd, eh? You just let me down off this ruddy tower, and I'll get it. Gives me the creeps."

"And just to make sure, you horrible specimen," said Toppy, "you'll sign a confession here and now that you took the money. We'll tear up the confession as soon as you hand us the cash. And it was £5 8*s.* 6*d.*, in case you've forgotten."

"Why, chums, a confession? Draw it mild. Don't you trust me?"

We all roared with laughter. I whipped out my note-book and pen, and handed them to him.

"Well, go on," said Toppy. "You *can* write, I suppose?"

"Now don't you go getting offensive. What d'you want me to write on this paper?"

"I'll dictate," said Toppy. "Ready? 'I, Joseph Seeds, hereby confess that—'"

"Go a bit slower, chum. I didn't have your education," muttered the Wart, laboriously writing.

" '—hereby confess that, in company with Johnny Sharp, I stole——' "

"Leave me out of it, buddy," came a soft, cold, poisonous voice from behind me.

We whipped round. Unheard, Johnny Sharp had come up the spiral stairs. He was standing now with his back to the door, and an expression on his face I had never seen there before. His right hand was in his coat pocket.

"Go on," he said. "Don't mind me. I just happened to be passing when I saw some of you kids at the church doors; and then you went in. So, having heard you was chasing my old buddy Jose around, I ses to myself, I wonder what they're up to: they wouldn't be going to chuck my old buddy, Jose, off the tower by any chance, would they?"

"Yurr, Johnny, these little perishers 've——"

"Because if they *was* going to chuck him off the tower," Johnny Sharp continued remorselessly, "I thought maybe I'd lend them a hand."

"Turn it in, Johnny," said the Wart. "You can't do this to me. Get me out of here. Let's go for these little——"

Johnny Sharp and his Slasher intervene

"Why should I? You were just writing a confession, weren't you? O.K. Go ahead. Only don't bring me into it, that's all. If you pinched some money off these kids, that's your look-out. Guess you'll have to give it back. Nothing to do with me."

The Wart swore a string of absolutely unprintable oaths, and made a lunge for his accomplice. But we were between the pair of them; and the next moment the Wart was huddling back against the coping, his face grey as yeast.

Johnny Sharp had flashed his right hand out of his pocket. He had a yellow suede glove on it, and his fingers held an open razor. He said, in a slow caressing sort of way:

"Now don't let's get rough. Somebody might hurt himself on my razor." Then suddenly his voice had an edge on it like the razor's. "Hand over that note-book, Jose, and move fast!"

Ted tried to snatch it first, but Johnny Sharp gave him a cuff that sent him reeling aside.

"Don't any of you interfere," the man warned. "Stand back over against the wall, the whole pack of you! Get moving!" His razor-blade flickered out like a snake's tongue, flashing in the sunlight. What could we do? He tore out of the note-book the page on which the Wart had begun to write his confession, and crumpled it in his pocket. With another flash of the venomous blade, he motioned the Wart to precede him down the stairs. He backed towards the door himself; then cocked his hat at a jauntier angle, grinned at us all, and said:

"Thanks for the memory, you kids. You've had a good game. But I shouldn't go on with it, if I was you. You forget about it, and little Slasher here will forget about it too. But if I have any more from you, if one of you should whisper a word of what's happened, little Slasher will make him sorry he was ever born. Got the idea? O.K. And just so that you can cool your silly little heads for a bit, I'm going to lock the door at the bottom of the stairs when I go out. Maybe that'll teach you not to interfere with Johnny Sharp again."

CHAPTER IX

THE SECRETS OF SKINNER'S YARD

"HE can't really *do* anything, can he?" Young Wakeley, in a slightly quavering voice, broke the silence which followed Johnny Sharp's departure.

"Of course he can't."

"Only carve us up into strips."

"The trouble is, we can't do anything either," said Toppy. "It's a stalemate."

Ted's Anglo-Saxon temper, smouldering for some time, now burst into flame. "We're *not* going to be beaten. We've got them on the run. Let's go through with it. Hands up anyone who's windy."

All our hands shot up as one man's. Ted grinned. "What I mean is, hands up who wants to chuck the whole business."

Not a single hand went up.

"Good show. We go ahead with our plans for the Commando raid on Skinner's Yard, then. We've got to get hold of that box. It's our last chance. And Johnny Sharp'll never expect us to take action so quickly: he thinks we're cowed by his threats."

"I bet he's wondering if we'll go to the police," said Nick.

"So we will. *When* we've got the box."

"What you don't seem to realise," said Toppy, whose mercurial spirits had sunk to zero, "is that we're prisoners on top of a tower. We're marooned. Isn't that so, Charlie?"

Charlie Muswell, who had gone down to see if Johnny Sharp had really locked the door at the bottom of the tower staircase, had just returned. "Yes, it's locked all right. I banged on it; but there can't be anyone in the Abbey to hear," he said.

As if by common consent we all moved to the side of the tower overlooking Abbey Green. A dizzy cliff of stone fell away beneath. People walking below were like ants dragging unwieldy shadows behind them.

"Yell for help," said Ted. "All together. Now!"

We gave a terrific yell. One or two people looked up, and waved. Just a jolly party of schoolboys having fun on the dear old Abbey tower. We yelled again and again. We made signs. We tried shouting in unison "*We're locked in! Open the door!*" But it was no good. Our words must have sounded like the confused babble of rooks to the people below.

"We might starve up here if no one comes," said young Wakeley.

"Don't be a wet. We'll get off all right."

"What? By parachute?" asked Toppy.

"Look here, why don't we all go down to the belfry and swing on the bells," exclaimed Nick. "That'd give the alarm."

"No need for that," said Peter Butts, who had been silent till now. "Trust your uncle Peter, the scientific wizard. We'll use a parachute, like Toppy said."

"Just one parachute for the lot of us?" sneered Toppy.

"Yes." Peter Butts turned to me. "Write a message for help in your note-book, George. Tear out the page and give it to me. Now will some kind lady or gentleman oblige me with the loan of a small penknife, some string, and a large handkerchief, preferably dirty."

We crowded round him. In less than a minute he had made a handkerchief parachute; the penknife was attached to the corners of it by four lengths of string and the message was firmly clasped by the blade.

"Now," said Peter. "Wait till a boy passes. Grown-ups wouldn't be bothered to wait for it to come down."

We waited about a minute. Then we saw an errand boy crossing the green with a basket on his arm. We yelled fit to burst. He looked up. Peter hurled the parachute as far ahead over the coping as he could. Leaning over we shouted again, all of us pointing like maniacs at the handkerchief parachute, which opened beautifully and went swaying and floating down towards the Green. The errand boy was gazing up at it, open-mouthed. It came to earth, looking no bigger now than a flake of snow, quite near him. I suppose of all the prayers which through the ages had ascended from the venerable pile of Otterbury Abbey, none was more fervent than the silent prayer which went up from us at this moment, that the errand boy should examine our parachute.

We watched him, in dead silence now, walk up to it. He dabbed at it with his foot. He looked up at us again. He made as if to move off. Then the bit of paper fixed in the penknife must have caught his eye, for he bent down. The next moment he was waving to us and running towards the Abbey door. We hustled down the winding stairs. Fortunately, Johnny Sharp had only turned the key of the door below, not taken it away with him. We were free! Toppy gave the errand boy half a Mars bar he had in his pocket, and ushered him politely out of the Abbey, asking him not to tell anyone about our being rescued from the tower, as it was against the school rules to go up it at all. Of course his real reason was that, if the boy talked, it might conceivably get round to Johnny Sharp and the Wart, and we wanted them to think we were still marooned

A message for help

up there. Then we settled down in the bell-ringers' loft for a last council of war. . . .

The narrative that follows, since I have no supernatural powers and cannot be in a dozen places at once, is compiled from the evidence of a number of eye-witnesses. But, even allowing for Toppy's well-known exaggeration, it is pretty accurate. At any rate, it satisfied Inspector Brook, sceptical though he was at the start.

When we left the Abbey, we broke up into pairs, so as to avoid giving the impression, if by accident we should meet the criminals, that the gang was still on their trail. Our instructions were to go home first and pick up any weapons we could muster, then to rendezvous at 17.30 hours in Ted Marshall's house. Ted had been rather against carrying weapons, but Toppy said they might come in handy if Johnny Sharp got free with his razor.

It was just as well that Rose had gone out to tea with Rickie after closing the shop that afternoon, because she might have put her foot down if she had seen the motley array of armed thugs who slipped into her yard at 5.30. Some of us had had considerable difficulty in accounting to our parents for dashing out of the house at such an hour, armed to the teeth. There were air-guns and air-pistols, water-pistols, clubs, wooden swords, wicked-looking sheath knives, scout ropes. Peter Butts turned up with a bow and a quiverful of arrows; in amongst the arrows there were three rockets which he'd been saving up for November 5th. Toppy produced from one pocket a bag of pepper and from another a Mills hand-grenade, which he'd swiped from the mantelpiece in his father's study; it was a souvenir of the 1914–18 war, and quite harmless without its detonator, of course; but Toppy said it might shake Johnny Sharp's morale if he lobbed it at him.

Ted had got the whole raid wizardly organised. At 17.40, two bicycle scouts were sent out with orders to station themselves one at each end of Abbey Lane. Their task was to note any suspicious characters entering Skinner's yard before the main body arrived at the Incident, and later to give warning on their whistles if Skinner himself should approach while Toppy and Ted were in the workshop. Simultaneously, Ted himself slipped round the corner into a public call-box and rang Skinner's place on the telephone. In a minute or two he was back: there had been no reply, which meant that the workshop was empty—Skinner had presumably gone home, as he generally did about 5 o'clock. We moved out, down West Street, singly, as far as possible concealing our weapons. By 17.50 hours we had infiltrated over the Incident and taken cover: the bicycle scouts had nothing to report. The task of this main body, which was under Peter Butts' command, was to cover the Commando party's retreat should they encounter opposition. If Ted and Toppy succeeded in breaking into the premises, and found the wooden box there, the rest of us would give them an armed escort to the police station. If they got hold of the box, but ran into trouble on the way out, the supporting troops would attempt to hold up or harass the enemy, while Toppy and Ted—whichever had the box—would dash for the end of the lane, leap on to one of the scout's bicycles, and pedal flat out for the police station.

Such were the plans. Just before 18.00 hours, looking up and down the lane to make sure there was no one in sight, Ted and Toppy rushed for the double doors of Skinner's yard. Four of us helped to hoist them over, then retired to cover again. We heard their footsteps moving stealthily across the yard and fading out of earshot. Then there was silence, a long long silence, broken only by the bumping of our hearts as we lay scattered over the Incident, our heads well down, our weapons ready. . . .

Ted and Toppy, pausing in the shadow of the high wall, looked round. It was an ordinary builder's yard, with stacks of timber, bricks, etc., lying about. On their right, facing the double doors and about 20–30 yards from them, was a sort of warehouse place, with a few windows high up, showing that it had two stories. At one side of this warehouse, at right angles to it, was an open shed, used for storing materials. They looked into this shed first. In the middle of it there was a cleared space, with oil on the floor: here, they reasoned, Skinner kept his lorry. And, as Toppy afterwards admitted, they were shaken to the wick to find the lorry was not there; because, unless Skinner had gone away for the night, it meant that he would be returning, any moment. So they hurried up with their reconnaissance.

The warehouse itself had a big wooden door in front, and a smaller one on the side facing the open shed. Both these doors were padlocked. Hurriedly they debated whether they should break one of the dusty ground-floor windows. They decided to do this only if no other way of getting into the workshop presented itself. Going round to the side again, they found a drainpipe and shinned up it, Ted in the lead. At the top, the warehouse roof sloped gently up to a glass skylight. The skylight, they rejoiced to see, was propped open.

We who were concealed on the Incident could not see them clambering up the mossy-tiled roof, because the angle of the building cut them off from us. But we heard a faint rattle, which was the sound of the skylight being opened higher to let them through.

It was lucky that they had borrowed a scout's rope from one of us, for the floor was a drop of twelve feet at least from the skylight. They made the rope fast to the iron support of the skylight, and climbed down. They were in the workshop all right. Benches, a lathe, carpentering tools, wood shavings, boxes of nails and screws—the whole place was littered with stuff, and they hardly knew where to begin their search. They decided to start at opposite ends of the place, and work towards each other. The search was thorough enough: they turned over all the litter on the benches and in the corners, they opened cupboards, they scuffled in heaps of shavings and in old sacks. Then at last, when they had pretty well ransacked the whole workshop, Ted opened a deep drawer in a bench in the middle of the room, and gave a cry of triumph.

"Here it is, Toppy!"

He pulled out a wooden box, exactly the same size as the one which had been stolen from him.

"Yes, that's it! Look for the mark! . . . Oh, *hell!*"

It wasn't the box. There was no cross scratched on the bottom of it.

"We'll take this with us, anyway," said Toppy. "It proves they made the box here."

"We've got to find our one, though!"

"But Skinner may be back any minute."

"We'll hear a scout whistling, if he does come. Let's get cracking. Search the rest of the building."

They ran to the door, and found a narrow, steep wooden staircase which brought them down to the ground floor. Here there were a number of empty wooden packing-cases ranged against the wall, and a few odd bits of furniture. Otherwise, in the murky light that came through the cobwebbed windows, the place seemed empty.

After giving this warehouse the once-over, Ted began, rather despondently, to open the drawers of an old dressing-table which stood, with several other pieces of furniture, near the outer door of the warehouse. One drawer stuck, after he had opened it, and in trying to force it shut again, he pushed the whole rickety dressing-table a little way back.

The descent into enemy territory

Where it had stood, there was a big trap-door in the stone floor!

Wild with excitement now, they pushed the dressing-table further back, so that the whole trap-door was clear; then laid hold of its iron ring and pulled. It came up easily, revealing—not, as they might have expected, a black hole beneath or a ladder, but a metal chute; the sort of thing you slide down on mats at a fun fair, only considerably broader. And the lifting of the wooden trap must have automatically thrown an electric switch, for the vaults to which the chute descended were brightly lit up.

Toppy and Ted looked at each other, speechless for a moment.

"This is it," whispered Ted at last.

"Yes, but what?"

"You game to try? I'll bet there's something shady goes on down there."

For the time being, they had both forgotten the real object of their raid, the wooden box.

"O.K. Try anything once," said Toppy, and getting on to the chute, he slid gracefully down it on his bim, with Ted close behind.

"The drop successfully accomplished, the airborne troops rapidly moved deeper into enemy territory." Toppy was talkative, as he always is when he's trying to conceal nervousness. "I say, it's an absolute robber's cave, Ted."

The vault, whitewashed, and lit by several unshaded electric bulbs, seemed cavernous, a whited sepulchre: its dimensions corresponded with those of the warehouse above. Like the warehouse, it contained an array of packing cases; but these were not empty, and there were far more of them, ranged against the walls. The air was dry down here, not dank and cold as it generally is in cellars. The pair moved over to a row of packing-cases. Toppy was still carrying the wooden box he had taken from the workshop.

"I say, Ted, do you notice anything peculiar about these packing-cases?"

"Yes, the labels have been torn off them all."

"I call it jolly sinister. I'm going to open one." And before Ted could say a word, Toppy was swarming up the chute on all fours. While he was gone, his companion cast round the vault. Near one corner he found a door. Opening this, he saw a dark passage in front of him. He went a few paces down this passage: by the light which came in from the vault, he saw a small wooden door on his left, in the passage wall. He tried this door, but it was locked.

The next moment, he heard a slithering sound behind him. Toppy was coming down the chute, holding a hammer and a big cold chisel he had borrowed from the workshop above. He advanced upon one of the packing cases, and began to open it.

"I say, it's not ours, you know," muttered Ted.

"I bet it's not Skinner's either," said Toppy, levering vigorously away at the lid.

There was a squeaking, rending noise as the nails gave way. Toppy took off some wrapping.

"What did I tell you? Skinner doesn't need these for the building trade."

The case was full of neatly-packed cigarette cartons.

"Crikey! The Black Market!" exclaimed Ted.

"What, no fags? Now we've got 'em!"

"We've got Skinner. But we haven't any evidence against Johnny Sharp except that we've seen him hanging about here. And we haven't got the box."

"Who cares about the box now?" said Toppy.

"I do. Nick still has the window to pay for. And there's his puppy——"

"Well, the box just isn't here."

"I want to try one more place." Ted led Toppy through the door into the passage, and pointed at the smaller door on their left. "Can you force that open with your cold chisel? It's locked."

Toppy set to work on it, hammering the chisel in near the lock and levering hard at it. Presently there was a splintering noise. The door sagged open. . . .

The main party was growing impatient. Toppy and Ted seemed to have been gone for ages, though in fact it was little more than half an hour. Discipline was relaxed: heads poked up from behind cover: one or two weaker spirits announced their intention of going home to supper if something didn't happen soon. I was just wondering if we oughtn't to send in some reinforcements to help with the search, when a distant throbbing came to my ears, then a frenzied series of whistle blasts from the end of the lane on our left; and a moment later Skinner's lorry hove in sight.

We only just had time to get our heads down, when it was upon us. Peering round the corner of my rubble-heap, I saw that Skinner himself was driving, and Johnny Sharp sitting beside him. The lorry drew up just beyond the yard doors. The Wart and an unshaven type leapt out from the back, unlocked a side door, went in and quickly threw the main doors open. As quickly, the lorry was backed in and the doors slammed shut again.

Ted and Toppy were trapped. . . .

"What the blue blazes is all this?" exclaimed Toppy, when they had found an electric switch inside the broken door.

They peered round the room in which they found themselves. It seemed to be fitted out as a laboratory. There was a bench; a table with bunsen burners on it; a sink; shelves with bottles of chemicals and various apparatus; a furnace; and, against the far wall, a large, complicated-looking metal press. But, what struck them as eeriest of all, was that everything was covered thick with dust and cobwebs.

"Miss Havisham's wedding-cake!" whispered Ted.

"Miss Havisham my foot!" Ted had opened a

drawer in the table, and taken out a wooden tray. The tray was full of half-crowns. He bounced one on the table, then bit it. "*Gosh,* Ted, this is where the Wart's half-crown came from! Look, it's soft, it's snide metal, just like I said it was when the Prune gave it us, only I was joking.* This is a coiner's den."

"Yes," Ted said excitedly. "And, judging by the cobwebs, they haven't done any coining for some time. I expect they couldn't get them right, make them hard enough——"

"More likely they found the Black Market more paying. Come on, Ted, this is where we exit pursued by a bear——"

"Pursued by a flying column of spiders, you mean——"

"We'll not need the box now. One of these half-crowns'll do the trick. . . . Stop! D'you hear anything?"

It wasn't the sentry's whistle they heard. They were too deep underground for this to have penetrated. What they heard was the roar of the lorry being backed up against the warehouse door overhead.

"The trap-door. Quick!" said Toppy.

They tore up the chute. But, as they reached the top, they saw the big warehouse door beginning to open. Toppy, who was ahead, managed to scramble through the trap; he flitted like a bat towards the staircase that led up to the workshop. In the mad *sauve-qui-peut,* his foot had accidently thrust against Ted, who slid a little way down the chute. By the time he had scrambled up to the trap-door again, the Wart and Johnny Sharp, their backs turned to him, were in the warehouse, only six yards away. Frantically, Ted tugged at the trap-door. It would be fatal if the men found it open. It slid

* We might have known this before. Did you guess, gentle reader? Anyway, try biting a real half-crown—your teeth won't leave any marks on it at all. [Author.]

back silently over his head. This was a respite at any rate. He careered down the chute, through the vault, into the passage beyond, bumping and bruising himself against the edge of a packing-case, for the sliding to of the trap had automatically switched off the electric lights in the vault. He paused a moment by the door of the coiner's den. There seemed to be no sounds of pursuit. Perhaps the roar of the lorry's engine had covered up the noise he made on the chute. He remembered he'd brought a pocket-torch. Switching it on, he turned off the light in the den, closed the splintered door, and crept off along the passage away from the vaults.

The passage took him about twenty paces. Then there was a flight of stone steps. Climbing up these, he found a blank wall, a grating set high up in it, and a small door. Desperately he tugged at its handle. The door was locked.

Ted knew it was only a matter of minutes before the gang realised something was wrong. The dressing-table moved out of position in the warehouse; the packing-case Toppy had opened; the splintered door of the coiner's den—there were too many signs betraying him. He sat down on the stone steps, his head in his hands, trying to steady his nerve. There was only one hope—that the gang would go upstairs first, find the scout-rope dangling from the workshop skylight, and assume that their birds had flown. But would Toppy have the sense to leave the rope there? Wouldn't his instinct be to remove this indication of their presence?

Then Ted caught at another straw of hope. Up above, in a cubby-hole off the workshop, there was a telephone. Perhaps Toppy had had time and sense enough to ring up the police before making his escape. If the gang found him, Ted determined that he would play this card, even though it might only be a bluff.

Even as he made this decision, he heard footsteps approaching along the passage, and a voice—the soft, cold voice of Johnny Sharp—saying "Come out! Come on out! And no tricks."

CHAPTER X

GRAND ASSAULT

"So it's you again," said Johnny Sharp, pushing Ted by the scruff of the neck into the vault. Skinner, the Wart and the fourth man were there, glowering at him.

"And what the hell are you doing on my premises?" thundered Skinner. His great shadow on the white-washed wall behind him seemed to swell and swell, like a blood-sucking spider's.

"I came to get back a box which these two stole from us."

Skinner moved ponderously up to Ted, and slapped him very hard across the face, twice. Ted's nose began to bleed.

"You keep a civil tongue in your head," said Skinner. "Better not start saying things about my friends. It ain't healthy, see?"

"It's not so healthy for you, either, having tons of stolen cigarettes down there."

Ted was like that. Once you got his blood up, he'd face a charging rhinoceros. Skinner's huge red face darkened; his piggy eyes were suffused with rage: he raised his fist as if to bash Ted through the stone floor.

"Just a minute," said Johnny Sharp, stepping between them. "Take it easy. Let me just ask *Mister* Marshall a question or two." His voice went smooth as melting butter. "You opened that case, did you?"

Ted nodded, white as death now. He feared this foxy creature a hundred times worse than Skinner.

Ted Marshall is introduced to the Slasher

"And was it by any chance you who broke into that room down the passage?"

Ted nodded again, holding his handkerchief to his bleeding nose.

"Had a good look round, eh?" pursued Johnny Sharp, in the same caressing voice.

"What's all this about a box?" asked the fourth man. "What's the kid talking about?"

"Shut up," said Johnny Sharp, without looking round at the man. "Now then, young Ted, did you crack this joint solo?"

"Crack the joint solo? What's that?" Ted looked as

stupid as he knew how. He was playing for time, thinking faster than he'd ever thought in his young life.

"Did you break in here alone," explained Johnny Sharp, in a put-on la-di-dah voice, "or were you accompanied by some other young gentlemen?"

"'Course he was alone," put in the Wart, "there's no one else here."

"I'm asking *Mister* Marshall."

Ted was silent. He'd made a heroic decision to alter his plan entirely. Obviously they'd not caught Toppy, nor could they have any proof that Ted had been accompanied in his raid. If he said that Toppy had been with him, had telephoned the police, he himself would probably be safe, but the gang would make a bolt for it at once and very possibly get away. If he said he'd broken in alone, they would have no reason to hurry, and Toppy might be able to get the police along in time to catch them.

"I'm waiting," said Johnny Sharp.

Ted remained silent. Don't tell your lie too quickly, or they'll suspect it's a lie, a voice seemed to say: let them drag it out of you. Johnny Sharp reached into his right-hand pocket, took out his razor, opened it, and made a few delicate passes in the air near Ted's face. A thin, high-shouldered shadow flickered grotesquely on the wall behind him.

"Little Slasher here always knows when little boys are telling the truth: little Slasher doesn't like being told lies. Come on, out with it! Were you alone?"

Ted nodded dumbly. He didn't have to *act* terror.

"Reckon this kid knows a bit too much," growled Skinner.

"I'm inclined to agree with our rough friend here," said Johnny Sharp, smiling at Ted and showing his discoloured teeth. "How lucky that nobody else knows you're here."

"No! You can't do that, Johnny," the Wart exclaimed. "He's only a kid."

Johnny Sharp, with finicky movements, closed the razor and replaced it in his pocket.

"Do what? I'm doing nothing. But, if a kid wanders in here and locks himself up by accident in one of Mr. Skinner's cellars, and if he happens to starve to death there—it's not my fault, is it? And who's to know, anyhow?"

Ted couldn't stand any more. He opened his mouth—to yell for help, to cry that the police would be here any minute. At that instant there was a terrific crashing and tinkling from the floor above, as a volley of stones smashed through the warehouse windows. . . .

The first we knew of what had happened in Skinner's warehouse was when we saw Toppy sprint out through the side door of the yard, which the Wart had left open. He was wrapping a handkerchief round his wrist; it had been badly grazed while he shinned down the drainpipe.

"They've got Ted," he gasped, running over to us on the Incident. "They must have got him. I only just managed to escape myself."

Breathlessly he told us about the crates of Black Market goods and the coiner's den.

"We must go to the police straight away," he said.

"*No*," came a firm voice. "We must rescue Ted first. The police might take ages to come." It was Nick, spoiling for battle.

"The police'll come quick enough when they see this

counterfeit half-crown," said Toppy. "Anyway, how can we rescue him? There are four men in there. We can't fight four men."

"Windy?" asked Nick, looking at him fiercely.

"Oh, if you put it like that—" Toppy's nerve was visibly returning. "O.K., we'll do it." He turned to me. "George, take a bike and sprint to the police station. Tell the scout to join us here. Take this half-crown and show it to the Inspector. And *hurry*!"

I shot off up the lane, half relieved and half ashamed to be missing the battle. I won't take up much time with my own part of the proceedings at this point, except to say it was darned lucky that Nick did persuade Toppy to launch an attack straight away. If they'd waited for the police, they'd have had to wait nearly twenty minutes, and the gang might have done Ted in. When I got to the police station, first I had to give my message to a duty constable; then I had to wait while it was passed on to the Station Sergeant; then *he* made me repeat the whole story—he was obviously sceptical to the back teeth, and I had to use all my famous eloquence to convince him this wasn't some kind of a rag. Luckily, Inspector Brook came in just then. He gave one look at the phoney half-crown, shot some questions at me, fast as machine-gun bullets, pretty well extinguished the Sergeant with a few blistering remarks about not knowing a bona-fide story when he heard one, telephoned madly in all directions for a few minutes, ordering roads out of Otterbury to be watched, then scooped up myself and three Bobbies into a police car, and tore off towards Skinner's Yard.

When we got there—but I'd better return to the grand assault, as it was related to me afterwards by some of the combatants. . . .

I must say, Toppy laid on a pretty masterly attack, considering he had to do it all on the spur of the moment. His plan was for the main body, under Peter Butts, to rush through the side door and fire a volley of bricks—there was plenty of such ammunition on the Incident—at the warehouse windows. They were to go on blazing away, while he himself got in again by the skylight, to try and rescue Ted while the gang's attention was diverted by the frontal attack. Nick said he was jolly well going to climb the drainpipe too and help rescue Ted: so that was that. Peter Butts was ordered to hold up the enemy's retreat, by any means in his power, till the police arrived. But, if he heard a whistle from inside the building, he was to lead the main body in and somehow put the fear of God into J. Sharp & Co.

An odd thing, worth recording, is that it never occurred to any of them to enlist the aid of one or two grown-ups who came along the lane while they were making their plans. Rickie had to admit, though, when we told him the whole story later, that they were probably right: either these passers-by wouldn't have believed them, or else they'd have said, 'Wait for the police,' grown-ups being a bit windy about winkling out gangs of desperate criminals.

Well then, to proceed with the battle. Toppy and Nick slid in through the side door. Presently a low call from the roof told Peter Butts that they had reached the skylight and found the road clear—there'd always been a possibility that one of the gang might have removed the rope from the skylight. Peter led his men in a dash over the lane and through the side door. Once in the yard, they sent their first volley through the warehouse windows. Then Peter had a bright idea. Ordering his men to cease fire for a moment, he leapt forward to the lorry which was still backed up against the main warehouse door, opened the bonnet, and tore out the leads to the sparking plugs. The enemy's transport was thus immobilised.

Meanwhile, Charlie Muswell and three boys with air-guns had made a flanking movement over to the shed, from which they could cover the side door of the warehouse. No sooner had Peter got back across the yard to his detachment, when the livid face of Skinner appeared at one of the broken windows. A well-judged shot with a half-brick made him withdraw it hastily....

Ted had been as startled as his captors by the smashing of the windows above, otherwise he might have got clean away from them while they were still cursing and swearing, which they did copiously. Then Johnny Sharp told the Wart to keep a grip on Ted till he and the man Skinner had found out what was happening. Ted knew, of course, that the breaking windows must be the start of an attempt at rescue, and that it wasn't the police. If only he could get up to the floor above, he might have a chance to elude the gang. Asking the Wart to let go of his arm while he took out another handkerchief to mop his nose (which had actually stopped bleeding by now), he suddenly ducked away and rushed up the chute. The Wart caught him again before he could dash out into the yard, but at least he was in the warehouse now.

He heard Skinner at the window, saying "Gaw blank my blank eyes! It's a crowd of blank blank kids!" —the blanks stand for unsavoury language with which the censor would not allow me to sully my page. And he saw Skinner jerk back his head, closely pursued by a half-brick.

Johnny Sharp called out something about 'the

underground passage.' Skinner bawled that he was going out to settle those blank blank kids first. Then the door at the far end of the warehouse opened and Toppy stood there, with Nick just behind him.

"Stick 'em up, the lot of you!" he said. "It's a cop!"

Skinner, shaking his head like a maddened bull, turned upon him. Toppy pulled the hand-grenade from his pocket, pretended to take out the pin, yelled "Run, Ted, run for your life!" and bowled the grenade along the floor towards the group at the other end of the warehouse.

The Wart gave a high whimpering scream. He released Ted and hurled himself through the main door out into the yard, where four boys at once wrapped themselves round his legs, dragged him to the ground, and in a minute had him trussed up with a scout rope.

The fourth man, the unshaven type, also lost his nerve. He dodged the rolling grenade and ran slap past Toppy and Nick before they could tackle him, out of the door by which they had entered. Charlie Muswell's chaps saw him emerge from the side door of the warehouse. They drew a bead on him with their air-guns and Charlie shouted to him to stop. But the fellow seemed deaf and blind with panic. He swerved round into the front yard, three air-gun pellets whizzing past his ears, broke right through Peter Butts' cordon, some of whom were engaged in sitting upon the Wart's head and tying him up, and got away. He was captured by the police two days later, incidentally, because we were able to give an accurate description of him: Charlie Muswell and Ted attended an identity parade and at once picked him out from the row of ill-favoured types lined up there.

Meanwhile, inside the warehouse, the situation had somewhat deteriorated. Before Ted had time to jack

The battle in Skinner's Yard

off, Johnny Sharp seized him and dragged him down behind the heap of old furniture. Skinner by no means lost *his* nerve. He bent down, fielding the rolling grenade, fumbled it, picked it up cleanly the next time and threw it out of the window.

There was a moment's involuntary pause, while he and Sharp waited for it to explode.

"Sucked in again!" shouted Toppy. "It was only a dummy!"

Skinner turned, mad with rage, and dashed at him. There's no doubt he'd have beaten Toppy to a pulp if he'd laid hands on him, for he was a desperate man by now. Toppy dodged the first charge. Nick tried to trip the man up, but was sent flying against the wall. Johnny Sharp, who still had a tight grip on Ted, didn't improve his accomplice's temper by calling out, "Can't you get him, you blundering fool?"

Skinner advanced upon Toppy again, more slowly now, his long arms dangling like a gorilla's, the fingers curled. Toppy, who had taken something else out of his pocket, slowly retreated. For a moment or two they circled. Then Skinner, roaring, made a dash and grab at him. Toppy's right arm came up. He flung the bag of pepper full in Skinner's face. He side-stepped neatly, avoiding the flail of Skinner's great arms. Skinner gave a howl of agony. He blundered on, his hands covering his face now, the fingers scrabbling at his eyes as if he would tear them out, so hideous was the pain of the pepper. He floundered blindly towards the yard door, felt the cooling air from outside, banged into the tail of the lorry, felt his way round it—and for some time felt no more: for young Wakeley, who had crept up into the lorry's cabin and found a heavy spanner lying on the seat, saw Skinner groping his way along the side of the lorry, leant over and brought the spanner down on his head. Skinner subsided like a deflating balloon. He too was tied up hand and foot.

The rest of the main body came pouring through the door, in answer to the whistle which Toppy had been too busy to blow till now. What they saw was not pleasant. Johnny Sharp, his razor out, was forcing Ted towards the trap-door.

"Hold it, you!" he snarled at them. "If one of you moves, I'll slash him. His own mother won't know him. Put those toy guns down, or I'll slash him!"

He would have too. He was a menace, that Johnny Sharp—a cold, cruel snake—and the boys stood there, as if hypnotised by him, lowering their weapons.

"Keep still, you, or I'll——" he warned Ted, who was writhing in his grasp. Ted went rigid. "Now, get down the chute!"

At that moment, a small figure hurtled out at Johnny Sharp from behind a stack of furniture, and fastened upon his right arm. It was Nick, who had managed to edge closer and closer, along the wall against which Skinner had flung him. On a day of heroic deeds, this was the most heroic. Seeing Nick struggling desperately to keep his grip on the wrist of Johnny Sharp's razor hand, hearing the sobbing breath as he was swung and battered against the furniture, the rest of them, led by Ted who had wriggled free from the man's grasp, got back their nerve and charged. It all happened in a few seconds. There was a clatter as Johnny Sharp let his razor fall to the ground. He shrugged his shoulders and went still. Nick, thinking he had surrendered, loosened his grip. The next instant he was sent flying against a packing-case, the edge of which cut his head open, and the trap-door was slammed in the attackers' faces as Johnny Sharp dived down the chute.

Ted kept his head well in this crisis. He told Charlie

Muswell to stay behind with his men and look after Nick till the police turned up. The rest were to follow him in the pursuit of Johnny Sharp. They would try to get a message back to Charlie as soon as they made contact with the enemy again.

So, when we arrived a few minutes later in the police car a dramatic spectacle met our eyes. Skinner's yard looked like a battlefield. Bricks and broken glass everywhere. On the leather seat taken out of the lorry's cab, his head tied up with bloodstained handkerchiefs, lay the still unconscious form of Nick Yates. A few yards away, very far from unconscious (they were swearing away as steadily as a stream of dirty water from a tap) lay Skinner and the Wart, lashed up in an absolute cocoon of rope, with three air-guns trained steadily upon them.

"One of them's got away," shouted Charlie. "Ted and Toppy have gone after him."

Inspector Brook wasted no time on routine questions. He strode over to Nick, gently felt his head, tried his pulse.

"Have you sent for a doctor?"

"No. Not had time yet. He's our only serious casualty," replied Charlie.

The Inspector sent a constable running to the telephone. He detailed another to keep an eye on Skinner and the Wart. Taking the third constable with him, he hurried into the warehouse. I followed them in, and down the chute. Inspector Brook gave one look into the crate which Toppy had forced open. He muttered something about "right under my nose—and it took a gang of kids to find out." Then he went down the passage, stuck his nose into the coiner's den, came out again, ran up the steps and found the door at the far end ajar.

"Suppose he got out this way. Come along."

Back in the yard outside, he took a brief look at the lorry. The men had had no time to unload it, of course: it stood there, stuffed with stolen goods for the Black Market, damning proof of their guilt.

"Anything to say?" asked the Inspector curtly.

"It was that —— Sharp who put me up to it," growled the recumbent Skinner.

"Well, that can wait. We'll pick him up soon enough. Hello, what d'you want?"

Young Wakeley had whizzed into the yard. "Message from the Commander," he said breathlessly. "Johnny Sharp—I mean the enemy—contacted in Dog Street—moving north-west—believed aiming to retreat across river."

The Inspector's mouth twitched slightly. "Does your—er, Commander wish for reinforcements?"

"You bet he does."

"Hmm. Seems to have done all right without them so far. However . . ."

He told off two of his constables to take Skinner and the Wart to the police station. Then we had to wait a minute or so for the doctor to arrive, and what seemed like an hour while he examined Nick's head, and the third constable, at his request, rang for an ambulance.

"Is he bad, sir?" asked Charlie anxiously.

"Not too bad. He'll get over it, with a thick head like his." And he winked at Nick, who had now recovered consciousness.

"Is Ted all right?" Nick managed to ask.

The Inspector, who seemed to have entered thoroughly into the spirit of the affair, bent over him and answered, "Yes, my lad, he's all right. He's just—er, mopping up the last pocket of enemy resistance."

Nick closed his eyes again, beaming all over his face with satisfaction.

Somehow Charlie and his three men, young Wakeley, myself and the Inspector all piled into the police car: the third constable took the wheel; and we accelerated hard for Dog Street and the River Biddle. . . .

Ted, leading the main party down the chute and across the vaults below, had been pretty sure that Johnny Sharp would try to escape by the door at the end of the underground passage—the one he himself had found locked. So they wasted no time in combing the vaults, but ran down the passage. Sure enough, the door was open now. Johnny Sharp must have been badly rattled or he'd have locked it again from the outside: or perhaps he thought we'd had enough, and wouldn't try to pursue him any further.

They bundled out through the door and found themselves in Pole Lane: this runs parallel with Abbey Lane, part of the oldest quarter of Otterbury. The leaders, looking swiftly up and down the lane, just caught a sight of the quarry before he turned a corner, just had time to see that he was holding his left wrist with his right hand.

"Gosh, look, he's wounded!" exclaimed Ted, pointing at some blood-spots on the narrow pavement. "He must have gashed himself accidentally during the struggle with Nick."

"Come on, the bloodhounds!" Toppy yelled, and the whole body surged off up the lane.

"No shooting!" called Ted, who is a law-abiding type for the most part. "It's not safe in the streets. Just keep on his tail!"

At the corner, they saw him again, about two hundred yards ahead—a high-shouldered figure walking rapidly away, still holding his left wrist, but jerking his head amicably at one or two passers-by just as if he were out for an innocent evening walk. Unfortunately, he glanced over his shoulder at this point, saw the vanguard of the pursuit, and dodged away into a side street.

It was no use trying to shadow him unobserved any longer. Ted ordered his party to go flat out after the fugitive, blowing their whistles and kicking up all the shindy they could, hoping that the alarm would gather a crowd which might hold up Johnny Sharp's retreat. But there weren't many people this evening in these back streets, and those who were about seemed to think the boys were just a gang of kids making a nuisance of themselves, and gave them some black looks.

Not that they noticed black looks. They were too busy trying to follow the trail of the blood-spots. Sometimes this trail disappeared; then, casting ahead, they found it again, just as they had found Nick's chalk-marks earlier in the day. The blood-spots told a clear story. Johnny Sharp must have cut himself deeply, for every now and then the pursuers saw thick splashes of blood on the pavement, where he had broken into a run and the blood had come out faster; and next, when he had slowed down and tightened the handkerchief again over the wound on his wrist, the blood-trail ceased.

Finally, the pursuers swung round into Dog Street—a long, narrow street with no side turnings, which leads to the allotments and the river, and comes out at the very place where we had caught the Prune fishing. Ted sent young Wakeley back to Skinner's yard with the message. The rest of them passed on down the street, and spread out across the allotments, where one ancient man leant on a fork and shook his fist at them for treading all over his vegetables.

Our artillery in action

Half-way across the river, in an ex-R.A.F. inflatable dinghy like the one the Prune had used for fishing, sat Johnny Sharp, paddling frantically. The boys lined the bank. The boathouse was closed for the night now, padlocked. This dinghy must have been left out by accident—a stroke of luck for Johnny Sharp. It was too late to go back and cross by the bridge and cut him off. Lined along the bank, the boys began firing at him. Pellets fizzed into the water round the dinghy, puckering it like a gust of rain. Johnny Sharp raised an arm to protect his face, and the dinghy slewed off its course. Then he started paddling again, his face queerly expressionless in spite of the snarl in which the effort to move faster had fixed his thin lips.

"Which of you can swim?" Ted snapped. He was seeing red all right. He'd really have jumped in and swum after that desperate criminal if Peter Butts hadn't called out:

"Just a mo! Let's try this first."

He had taken the rockets out of his arrow-quiver, and stuck their wooden sticks horizontally into the steep river bank. Quickly aiming one at the enemy, he lit the fuse. There was a whoosh, and the rocket streaked away, high over Johnny Sharp's head. The man's face became convulsed with terror, as Peter, very carefully and deliberately now, adjusted the angle of his next rocket, sighting along it at the dinghy, which was now only twenty yards from the opposite bank. Johnny Sharp bawled something, nobody cared what. They were waiting in dead silence for the fuff and whoosh of the second rocket. It went for Johnny Sharp like a stab of lightning, skimming the water. He yelled, jerked away, overturned the dinghy, and disappeared under the water.

"Help, I can't swim!" he whined, his head emerging again.

A figure shot past the boys and dived in. It was a constable. The police car had arrived.

CHAPTER XI

GENERAL SALUTE

THE next morning, at prayers, the Headmaster announced that the whole school was to assemble in the Great Hall at 11 a.m. I suppose we all had a sort of hang-over from the events of the previous day: to me, at any rate, they seemed like a dream; and the Headmaster's ominous announcement—because the whole school assembling in the Great Hall generally meant big trouble—didn't strike a very reassuring note. A hideous thought shot into my mind: what if we were wrong all the time? Suppose Skinner and the Wart and Johnny Sharp were in fact perfectly innocent, and there was some simple explanation for the apparently damning evidence found at Skinner's yard? My word, we should be in the soup! We'd be in an absolute hell-broth of a witches' cauldron.

I put this notion to Ted, as we went in to the first lesson.

"Don't be so wet," he said. "The Inspector'd have clapped the lot of us in jail if——. No, what I'm worried about is the window Nick broke. We still haven't got the money for it."

At 11 o'clock we trooped along to the Great Hall. As you can imagine, rumours of what we'd done the day before were flying all over the school, many of them wildly exaggerated, and a number of silly asses greeted Ted and Toppy with coarse gestures intended to represent the details of public execution.

Presently the masters filed on to the dais in cap and gown, and sat down, trying to look dignified. Then the

Headmaster swept in. With him, to our dismay, was Inspector Brook. The Headmaster put him in a chair on his right; then rose, hitching his gown up with his left hand, and presented to the school a countenance dark as a dust-storm looming up over a desert horizon. I swallowed hard. Toppy, I noticed, had his fingers crossed.

"I have assembled you this morning," began the Headmaster, "for a—hum-ha—an unprecedented reason. Never in my long experience, both as an assistant master in various——"

"Oh lord, he's off," murmured Toppy. "Wake me up in an hour's time!"

"——have I heard such an extraordinary story as Inspector Brook told me last night. It would seem that certain boys in the Junior School saw fit to spend the week-end and the extra whole holiday in activities beside which the outrages of Chicago gangsters would look, would—er, hum, chrm'm——."

The H.M. appeared to choke with indignation. I tried to catch Rickie's eye, but he was leaning back in his chair on the dais, with his hand shading his face. The H.M. sipped his glass of water and started off again.

"Not only did they virtually hold the town to ransom, by organising various—er—side-shows and money-making enterprises—I am given to understand that shoe-shining, shoe-shining *in public* by King's School boys, was one of these discreditable occupations——"

"You bet it was," murmured Toppy. "*And* we cleaned yours, *in* public."

"——and in general they made a scandalous nuisance of themselves, all over Otterbury, with their absolutely unauthorised collecting of money. This, to be sure, I should have been prepared to overlook, since I have reason to believe that the money was collected, however misguidedly, for a charitable object—for the, ha-hum, in short, for the relief of one of their schoolfellows. *But*—" the H.M. drew himself up to his full height, and his black gown swirled around him like a thundercloud "—but these childish pranks pale into insignificance beside what happened yesterday. I cannot trust myself to speak about this. I will ask Inspector Brook to address you. But first, will every boy who was in any way concerned with the—er—the attack on Mr. Skinner's premises step up on to the platform here."

We shuffled up, and were made to stand in two rows on the left of the dais. It was worse than my worst forebodings.

The Inspector fastened Ted and Toppy with a frosty eye. Then he turned to the school.

"It's never a good thing to take the law into your own hands," he began briskly. "We policemen are here to enforce the law—it's our job. So, next time any of you get into trouble, or have genuine cause for suspecting somebody else of criminal activity, I hope you'll come to us. But I hope there won't be a next time. We in Otterbury have a pretty clean sheet, and we should be proud of it. Now these boys here got up a collection—incidentally, I had some complaints from our townsfolk about their methods, but I decided to turn a blind eye on it—it seemed to me fairly harmless. But then the money they had collected was stolen from one of these boys. And, instead of coming to the police, they decided to do some detection off their own bat."

The Inspector paused, coughed dryly, and took a swig out of the tumbler in front of him.

"So they got into deep waters. I've had a talk with one of them, Edward Marshall, and it's quite clear to me "—his frosty eye seemed to twinkle for a moment—"it's quite clear to me that Scotland Yard couldn't teach some of you youngsters very much about the elements of criminal detection."

The school was hushed—not a cough or a shuffle as they drank in the words of this remarkable man.

"Yes, it was a very pretty piece of investigation. But, having worked out their theory and collected evidence to support it, these enterprising boys still did not come to the police. I don't know whether they thought we'd eat them." (Polite laughter). "Anyway, they decided to go after the suspects. They needed one more bit of evidence to clinch their case, or so they thought. In order to get this—it was a certain wooden box—they planned and carried out a felony. They broke into the premises of a—er, of a respected citizen of this town, whom they had no reason to suspect of complicity in the original robbery. This was serious enough—— "

Inspector Brook paused again, while a buzz of astonishment and wild surmise went up from the assembled school.

"But not only did they break into private premises. Marshall and Toppingham—and all these boys on my left here were also accomplices before the fact—started a gun battle. The police can charge them with carrying lethal weapons with intent to wound, breaking and entering, intimidation, assault and battery, shooting at certain fellow-citizens, discharging rockets at same, and—er, in short, these are just a few of the charges to which they may have laid themselves open."

By now, the school was simply petrified with amazement.

"Yesterday evening, acting on information received"—the Inspector's mouth twitched again—"I proceeded to Skinner's yard. There I found, amongst

The Inspector sums up

other things, one of these boys, Nick Yates, lying unconscious with a broken head—he's well on the way to recovery now, the doctor tells me—and two citizens of Otterbury tied up with ropes and threatened by several boys with air-guns. I also found"—the Inspector paused dramatically—"I also found evidence that these citizens, together with one who was captured shortly afterwards—he was the—er—target for the rockets I have mentioned—and a fourth who is still at large, were receivers of stolen goods, distributors of the same through Black Market channels, and had at one time been engaged in coining counterfeit money."

Sensation in the Great Hall of King's School, Otterbury!

"I have to say that, but for the—er—somewhat unorthodox activities of my young friends here, the crimes of this gang might never have been discovered," went on the admirable man, beaming all over his face now, "and that, in view of this, the police do not propose to press against you young ruffians any of the charges I have spoken of."

The School began to cheer, but Inspector Brook raised a large hand. Looking straight at us now, he continued:

"Furthermore, I have to say that, after hearing the full story, I consider you all acted with resource and initiative and courage. I won't pick out any one of you, except perhaps Nick Yates—he's in hospital and I can't make him blush from here. He tackled a very dangerous man. It was a brave thing. A good show by all of you. A credit to the school. As a token of the police's gratitude, I'm going to ask an old friend of mine—he's a Detective Inspector at Scotland Yard—to show you over the place one day in the holidays: you might be able to give him an idea or two. And one of the firms whose stolen goods you helped to find—it's a chocolate-making firm—I've been in touch with them and they've told me to distribute a pound of chocolate to each of you."

By this time the cheering from the school was so deafening that we could hardly hear what the Inspector was saying. He mopped his brow. while the din subsided.

"That's about all I have to say. Except that, when you young terrors next embark on a gun battle with a gang of crooks, you might let me in on it. *And*, if ever again I hear of you so much as raising a water-pistol against anyone, I'll clap you in the cooler as sure as eggs are eggs! But seriously, no more taking the law into your own hands, see? Promise?"

We promised fervently. The Inspector sat down. I noticed Rickie lean over to the Headmaster and whisper in his ear. The H.M. rose. He was looking as pleased as Punch.

"We are grateful to Inspector Brook for talking to us, and for taking so lenient a view of your conduct. Since you seem to have broken half the windows in Otterbury, we'd better forget about the one which Nick Yates broke: the School authorities will pay for it. Now go along quietly to your classrooms. QUIETLY!"